Zachariah Tree [...] ill-ers, getting close enough to eat the coach's dust. Entering a high-walled gap, the rumble of the wheels echoed from the granite walls, and the rig rolled from the deep shade of ravine into glaring sunshine.

Then a slamming blast of a ten-gauge scatter gun boomed out.

"Damn!" shouted the hangman. Griswold's blast had flown wild, and Tree was alive. He bent low across the saddle bows, and spurred his mount into a last tremendous dash to within a few yards of the coach. Now Tree leaned and launched himself, grabbing onto the boot behind the racing wheel. Using every ounce of his strength, he hauled himself up on the vibrating cargo brace and locked a hand on the solid baggage bar. With another powerful pull, he rolled onto the roof, arms and legs splaying awkwardly.

The jehu, Haldane, glanced around and shouted down to his pard inside, "Griswold, the bastard's climbed aboard!"

Then, with a bursting crash, the boards exploded upward, blowing the stage roof open in a hail of double-aught buck.

"I got the bastard!" roared Sam Griswold. "Blew him off'n the roof and plumb to hell!"

Other Books in **THE HANGMAN** series:

**#1: Quick Drop**

# THE HANGMAN

## BLOOD KNOT
### Craig Foley

A DELL BOOK

Published by
Dell Publishing
a division of Bantam Doubleday Dell
Publishing Group, Inc.
666 Fifth Avenue
New York, New York 10103

The trademark Dell™ is registered in the U.S. Patent and
Trademark Office.

ISBN: 0-440-20374-0

Printed in the United States of America
Published simultaneously in Canada

September 1989

10 9 8 7 6 5 4 3 2 1

# BLOOD   KNOT

To
Marilyn

# Chapter One

The battered Concord stagecoach swayed crazily behind the horses charging up the mountainous grade. The road had been climbing for hours, leaving behind the butte-studded open lands below for the boulder-strewn approaches to the Black Hills massif. Although the tree cover remained sparse on the rock mounds on every side, scents of pine wafted on the breeze, sweetening the swirling dust.

The jehu on the box worked his whip and a curse-spewing tongue to keep the team moving and the miles unfolding. The idea was to reach Deadwood before nightfall.

Speed was important now because the route ahead was wicked traveling, too cragged and winding to attempt at night. For the moment, though, the vast dome of Dakota sky canopied the stage with cloudless blue. Jackrabbits bounded in roadside grass. A hawk soared.

Inside the coach, talk between the two passengers with loud voices and strong views had grown noisier as the warm spring afternoon wore on.

"Damn," declared the drummer. "'Twas the finest hanging ever, down in Silver City!" The fellow wearing the frayed suit and scraggly mustache was determined to outtalk the crag-faced preacher man.

"They hang 'em no place in the world like they hang 'em in Abilene," the Bible thumper vowed. "No, no mercy, none at all! Just the noose and the long, slow pull! Pretty to see, sinners sent down to hell! Praises be! They kick, they choke, they bleed!"

"Bleed?" the drummer half shouted. "Why, that time in Virginia, the drop, it sheared the culprit's nose off! And di'n the townsfolk cheer plenty then!"

"Young braggart!" The older man seemed about to leap, but the coach took a jolt and threw him back beside his seat mate. The third passenger was not part of the discussion. In fact, he had said little since he had boarded clear back at Pierre. Nor did he look like a man given much to talk, certainly not loose talk that could accomplish nothing.

Above middling height, but not by much, he had an air of quiet strength about him. Strong shoulders bulged the black serge of his frock coat. His clean-shaven face, with its jutting jaw, was controlled like a practiced poker player's.

Ignoring his traveling companions and rolling with the coach's motion, he watched the terrain as it flowed past outside the open, breezy window.

It wasn't that he admired scenery. He simply viewed pointless debates by those no better than fools with distaste.

"Nobody's harder on the rustlers and owlhoots than Nevadans!"

"They choke 'em vicious as can be, down Kansas way!" A pause for effect. "Even poisoners! Even females! Ever seen a fat ol' gal thrash, shit, and twitch? Huh? Hot damn!"

The man in the black coat yawned. The team was slowing down. The coach jarred and swayed less at the reduced speed. They were easing through a bend around a thrusting cliff, and there, under tall jack pines, stood a way station. Fresh horses waited in a pole corral. In front of the neat log structure, dust devils played.

"Whoa, consarn ye, animules! Whoa!" As he applied brake, the driver jerk-sawed his reins. Both the team and rig rolled to a halt. Within, the disputing men, unnoticing, went on with their exchange. The drummer was making a particularly interesting point, he believed.

"I've seen all kinds, both legals and lynchings. Trees, scaffolds, telegraph poles — whatever's to hand. Hoist 'em high, and let 'em dangle! Rid the countryside of scum, by God!"

# THE HANGMAN

"You ain't c'rect, takin' the Lord's name in vain!"

"The hell, you say?"

"Gents, if you'll excuse a feller a call of nature?" The man in black jammed his flat-top Stetson on his head capped with sorrel hair. He squeezed between the drummer and the preacher, pushed open the coach door, and stepped to the trampled hardpan. In doing so, he met up with the driver, a grizzled oldster with a face like worn saddle leather.

The jehu frowned as he scanned the rutted compound. "Now, where the hostlers gone? Here's a coach all a-waitin' for a team! Them lazy no-accounts!"

At that instant, from out back came a cry and gunshots. Hurtling from the wall's concealment came a thin figure clad in a baggy shirt and dark pantaloons. Smoke seemed to be pouring from his head because the man's hair was afire. Long inky black hair in a braided queue slapped his shoulder blades as he ran. The wails from his lips turned to wild screeches. Behind him appeared two white men wielding six-guns and throwing shots.

The Chinaman, scared witless, sprinted straight at the coach. "Hold on there!" the man in black called out. The Chinaman answered by screaming protests in his native tongue.

The man in black tripped the Chinese as he passed, leaped atop the struggling form, and stifled the flames with his hat. In a few seconds the fire was out. "Take care of him!" he barked to the driver, then surged back to his feet, and bounded at the pair of sweating swing-station hands. Both were trying to get past him to the foreigner they were bent on tormenting.

"Out of our way, there! That chink come to scrounge and thieve!"

"No call for you to mix in this, mister. We caught the slant-eye on comp'ny property, right enough, and we'll give him his deserts!"

The man in black stood his ground in front of the angry pair. "Got proof that he stole something, have you?"

"Hell, no! And don't need none, neither — 'cepting his yeller hide. All them people know is stealing." The lankier of the two fellows swung a fist at the stranger in black. Then, when his own mouth felt an answering blow, the man reeled back at the force, colliding with his pard. Now both of the stage line's hostlers, paled at the onslaught, sought to backpedal, but the stocky passenger waded in with his arms pumping, driving bunched knuckles to the men's midsections and faces.

"Hey, mister, I said we meant no harm," the larger of the two spat out between bloody, split lips. "He's a goddamn coolie. It ain't like he was people. They're animals, his kind! We was only —"

The man in black interrupted by grabbing the babbling man's shirt. "Appears to me there's no call for torturing. Don't make no difference if it's white or Chinese folks."

"Shit," the bullet-headed jasper grunted, nursing his bleeding nose. But his companion with the flushed red face snatched up a short length of harness chain from the ground and whipped it around fast.

The man in black stepped inside the vicious swing, blocked it, and sledged a rock-hard fist against the attacker's cheek. His head snapped back, and the hostler went to his knees, drooling blood. "Damn, mister, I still say this ain't your business. This is our country and his kind's floodin' all Dakota Territory!"

"And they got the right, same as you, to homestead and stake mining claims, not just work for penny wages." The Asian's defender blew on his knuckles to ease the cuts, then beckoned the young yellow-skinned man to him. He came on hesitating, slippered feet, his expression still a mask of fright.

"Now for a couple of polite apologies."

"We don't know no slant-eye lingo," Bullet Head grumbled.

The stranger unbuttoned his coat, exposing his Colt .44.

"Oh, awright, mister, awright! Chinaman, we had no call to torch your pigtail."

"Now, your sidekick," the man in black demanded.

The stage driver watched grinning while the man with the red face blurted the same few words. From the corners of his cool, gray eyes, the man in black noted the looks of the pair whose faces were framed within the stagecoach windows. There were other things of interest to them besides talk of grisly hangings.

"Now, unless I miss my guess, you boys still expect to draw pay from Wells Fargo Express. The stage you see standing there is getting further behind schedule by the minute. Reckon you can hump yourselves and get fresh horseflesh into harness before much longer?"

The two hostlers nodded.

"No hard feelings, then." As the hostlers hurried toward the corral, the black-clad man turned to the still-silent Chinese. "From all appearances, you ain't shook up all that bad. Mainly some singed hair, and that ain't pleasant, but at least you're alive. You need a ride into Deadwood?"

A violent shake of the head. "Won Lee, he no go to Deadwood town. Come away from there, walk ver' fast. Not good place, that place. Don't like it, Chinee dig for gold. Won Lee, he taking him other way."

The man in black grew suddenly thoughtful, and bobbed his jaw. "Then good luck to you, Mr. Won Lee." When the Chinese man had shuffled down the road and out of sight through the trees, he tugged the Stetson down and shrugged. "Now, for my appointment with that privy I spotted out back." He ambled off around the end of the cabin.

By now the battered men were changing the team, leading away the tired and sweat-flecked horses, and checking single tree chains and harness leather. The driver was leaning against the coach, watching the men work.

"Quite a fistfighter, the gent with them black clothes. Never woulda guessed it from his quiet manner," the preacher said.

"No, sir," agreed the drummer, "and that's for sure. Say, driver, he got him a name that you happen to know?"

The grizzled old fellow spat tobacco juice and grinned lopsidedly. "Why, I know that he's Zachariah Tree, none other — about the most famous professional hangman west of the Mississippi. Got his reputation for hanging straight and proper. Oh, there's some as are partial to dishing all the pain they can, but Tree does his job quick and clean. Learned his trade right, down in Texas, where he hails from."

The driver cocked his head and scratched his dome, then added an afterthought. "I reckon he's on his way to Deadwood on hanging business."

The newly hitched horses tossed their manes and danced in the traces. The driver hauled himself to the box and filled a hand with pebbles from his pocket to throw at the round rumps to settle them. Zachariah Tree reappeared and crowded into the Concord's close confines. He stretched his legs as much as possible, leaned back, and relaxed.

His two fellow passengers just sat in their seats and stared at the reclining hangman, too awestruck to talk.

The stage had tooled along the rugged road for quite some time before Tree began to wonder what had happened to the tedious conversation.

Well, he thought, if they had smoked the peace pipe, so much the better. It did let a man rest.

# Chapter Two

"I tell you, Zack, my boy, it was a nasty crime, and I was glad when the trial was over and done with. Acting as judge, I hadn't a qualm over condemning the guilty pair to die by the noose. And you and me go back a ways, Zack. You know I didn't just gavel the accused down on account of 'em having yellow skins and slanty eyes."

Tree studied the elderly chap in the baggy, threadbare Prince Albert jacket. His face had sunken in the years since Zack had last seen him. The man's papery skin had become stretched tight over his bones, but it still belonged to Judge Enos Depew. "I reckon that's c'rect," the man in black assured the old fellow.

The two sat in battered rocking chairs in the old magistrate's parlor. The dwelling had been thrown up using unplaned boards, like most buildings in the new boomtown of Deadwood. However, unlike many, it possessed a roof of real cedar shakes, not canvas, making it one of the few permanent buildings around.

The judge had been kept busy from the minute he'd come to the raw gold camp. Lots of infractions meant lots of fines, hence Depew's reasonably good living standard. He didn't need to squat out in the diggings or sleep in sugans on the stony ground, as did so many moneyless newcomers.

The great rush sparked by Colonel Custer's discovery of gold in the Black Hills had attracted its share of down-and-out scroungers. It had also brought in hundreds, and some said thousands, of dark-clothed, pigtailed Chinese.

Tree fished out the makings, including his small muslin sack of pungent Union Leader tobacco, and built a quirly. The problem of the Chinese was touchy all over the country, and he got the feeling it was especially so here. They were the hardworking people that had built the West's great railroads, but weren't so welcome where so many white people were pickaxing and placering, hoping to make fortunes of gold.

And now in Deadwood, Chen and Fong, two Chinese men stood convicted of foul murder by a jury. The victim that the pair were said to have knifed to death was the man who had sold them their gold claim. The weapon, an Oriental dagger with an unusual blade, had been found bloodstained in the accused men's stick-and-scrap-slab shack.

The motive: revenge — or at least that was how it had looked to neighboring miners and the local law. Tree hadn't met the marshal yet. When he first stopped by the jailhouse upon reaching town, he had found the marshal was out. So he had inquired of the "townie" left in charge, and afterward came straight over to pay this call on Depew. The old judge agreed entirely with the revenge theory, it turned out. It had been put forward at the trial that he had presided over, and it seemed to make sound sense.

Before an execution, Tree felt it his duty to probe the facts of the case. "I understand," he said now, "that the victim, a feller called Jones, cheated the Chinamen with the old salted-mine stunt. Enough to make any men mad, only these boys, Chen and Fong, got their evens by sending the trickster on down to hell." Tree shook his head solemnly. Human nature being what it was, such acts happened every day.

"You understand right, Zack. You understand j-just r-right." Then the burr in the old man's throat turned to a cough, and in no time he had a handkerchief to his mouth and spat plentifully. But when the trouble subsided, the pallor fled from the old man's face. He was able to continue talking.

"Marshal Wilmer hiked on over to the claim in question," Depew went on, "seen for himself what some of the prospectors was pointing out. Inside the short tunnel Jones had dug, one whole rock face was all a-speckled with bright gold color. But it didn't go deep down. 'Twas fine gold dust shotgunned at the wall. Oh, a neat job, but the kind you uncover soon if you're a hard digger. Alonzo Jones's mistake was, he didn't clear right out of these parts."

"And a knife found its way between his ribs."

"Now, Zack, who done went and told you that?"

Tree raised his head. "Why, the telegram I got, it explained — "

"Did it?" The old man fixed Tree with a rheumy gaze. "The victim was stabbed in the back, it's true, but he was poked and sliced all over with that curved blade. Holes in his neck, front, and sides, plus his guts spilled with a long, deep slash. Even Jones's arms and legs was cut up pitiful. When the body was found the morning after, there was plenty of puking."

"Where'd it happen?"

"Along a path 'tween Deadwood's saloon district and the pitched tent up a ravine where Jones rented them a bedroll. A dark stretch at night, and an empty one. Another fool thing, a man walking it by himself, that way."

As Tree puffed his quirly, gray smoke wreathed his head. Flies hummed. Dusk was settling in and fast. He was going to need to find a beanery and eat, and try again to waylay the Deadwood marshal. But he had a few more questions for old Depew, as well. "The knife must've made some peculiar wounds, but ain't it funny, suspecting those particular Chinese? They'd find the knife in their hut?"

"Of all the heathen hereabouts, which had the grudge, Zack? Sure, the miner vigilantes went direct to Chen and Fong. And tearing up their place, there the knife was, stuffed under one of their sleeping pallets. When the boys turned it up, Mike had him a job to do to stop a lynching."

"Mike?"

"Mike Wilmer, the Deadwood marshal."

"Oh, sure." Tree creaked the rocker forward and got up. "Well, glad for the palaver, Enos. Always good to find an old acquaintance where one happens to be. Especially in my trade."

A dry cackle of a laugh rang out. "Yeah. A hangman, he's got a lonesome trail if he's like you. You never did cotton to town bigwigs' shindigs, nor getting likkered up with the local lawdogs." The judge's gnarled hands gripped his chair, but he failed to rise. "Mind seeing your own self out, son? The o-old rheumatiz, t'day she's got me by the short hairs."

"Enos, I'll find my way just fine."

Zack Tree let himself out into the balmy mountain evening. Night birds called each other from the brush that sprang up everywhere along the slopes of the cut. The hangman headed back toward the crowded center of the town, where lamps shone through windows and holes in canvas roofs. In one of the improvised saloons or brothels, a tinny piano was having its keys tickled. A drunken shout lifted and was broken off.

It was business as usual in a wild frontier setting. Soon Tree trudged the boardwalk, surrounded on all sides by mining men looking to drink, gamble, or find a woman.

Yeah, Tree thought, the streets are lined with gambling houses. So's to relieve the boys of any heavy pockets. Natural. Lucky at the diggings, unlucky at the tables was the rule, it seemed. Gambling fever went hand in hand with gold fever.

When Tree reached the jailhouse he found a man loafing alone on the doorstep. "And might you be Marshal Wilmer?" he asked.

"Yeah, that's me."

"Uh . . . " The hangman moved closer. "Zachariah Tree, that's my handle. I came in on the stage."

"Deadwood town has been waiting on you, Mr. Hangman," said the man wearing the hammered copper star. "Come right on inside."

Mike Wilmer's office was as dirty as the lawman himself. The main difference was that the place was small, the man was large. A bulky figure with a paunch like an oats sack, he shambled rather than walked across the floor to a scarred oak desk.

Beside the desk, the marshal drew up to full height, thrust his chest out, and scrubbed his jaw with a sleeve. "I been out making the rounds of the saloons, Tree. Trouble from drunk gold hunters plagues us in the gulch. And I got to tell you, it didn't help, the time you took getting here. Plenty boys wanted to turn the murderers over to good King Lynch."

"I reckon the more peaceable-minded citizens thanked you for your trouble. They must want a proper, legal hanging."

"Because you got sent for?" Mike Wilmer scowled. "Pshaw! Weren't no peaceable citizens as wanted an outside hangman. Fetched you here on old Depew's say-so. This round, the codger could be right, though. Show the whole passel of slant-eyed monkeys hereabouts that even the gov'ment don't want them on the loose!"

"I ain't the government, exactly," Tree said. "Leastways, not except for this hanging of two jury-tried jaspers condemned for murder. And that ain't to do with a man's skin color."

Deadwood's law peered at the hangman with a surprised squint. Then the slack features went a bit slacker and gave way to a knowing look. "If you say so, Mr. Hangman. Hey, now you've come, why not have the neck-stretch soon? How 'bout tomorrow?"

"If I can examine the culprits tonight, sure. I take their weights and figure the length of drop." Mike Wilmer smiled. "Ain't nothing keeping us from it. The general store next door has him a set of scales. I'll just go borrow 'em. Meet you back by the pris'ners in a minute or so."

"See you then."

The badge toter plodded out the front, and Tree estimated he'd have more than a few minutes. No sense wasting it, he decided, and headed toward the back to begin his sizing of the

culprits. He strode through the doorless walk-
way and to the jailhouse rear, expecting a wall of
bars, complete with factory-patent door.

He was in for a surprise.

The town hadn't means or inclination to do
things the ordinary way. What confronted Zack
Tree was an eight-foot-square cage, homemade
by a blacksmith. The materials were hot-riveted
pieces of iron. The iron had been far from new,
and wore a coat of orange rust. Inside — and it
was hard to see well — two miserable humans
hunkered on the bare floor. In the cage's corner
stood a brown-streaked slops bucket, the source
of a disgusting stench.

"Chen and Fong?" Tree came straight to the
point. "You got to get to know me sooner or later.
I'm the hangman that'll be seeing you out of this
world, punishment for the crime you done. I
ain't the jury, nor one of the witnesses, and
haven't to do with the why of your fix. I hope
you can see that. I'm set to do my job, is all, and I
aim to do my best.

"Now, if I study on you boys' weights and the
tone of your neck muscles, I'll be able to drop
you fellers on the noose plumb clean. With as
little damage to your mortal remains as might
be. Savvy?"

Through the bars he glimpsed two pairs of
eyes returning his gaze. The faces were round
and yellow, but they held the same fear that a
white man's would under the circumstances.
But there was another emotion as well: puzzle-
ment. The truth dawned on Tree in a rush. The

men had barely, if at all, understood what he had told them.

Strangers in a strange land, they didn't know the language. Likely, they knew no language at all well but their native Cantonese. And they had gone through a rough-justice, frontier-style, American trial, and came out under sentence of death! Had they understood the things said on their big day in court, Tree wondered. Surely they knew they had been condemned!

And then Zack Tree's hesitation melted as he studied on the situation. What did it matter, really, that these two murderers may have missed some of the testimony leveled against them? From what he had heard, it was clear as hell, the things that had happened leading up to the violent death of Alonzo Jones.

Jones was a bad actor, right enough, who had cheated two would-be miners of the money that had paid for a claim. The ore-laced rock face that had been shown them later had proved to be a "plant," if a clever one. In the duped men's homeland, as in most places the world over, folks were used to righting wrongs as they saw fit.

Trouble was, it went against American law. So the citizens of Dakota Territory were making two killers pay the price for their deed.

The justice seemed plain.

"Ah, there you be, Mr. Tree." Marshal Wilmer bulled into the room gleefully. "Let's get right on with what you got do. Then we'll carry us a lantern on outside, and I'll show you our new gal-

lows." The lawman keyed open the massive pad-
lock on the cage door, swung it open, and
stepped back as he drew his Colt. "Now, you
monkeys, one at a time! The gent aims to look
you over! Move your tails!"

Tree went to work efficiently. It seemed the
Chinamen gauged Wilmer's voice tone, and the
meaning of his big .45.

# Chapter Three

The day had dawned fine for a hanging or a picnic — or both. By ten o'clock that morning, the appointed hour for the execution, the wide main street of Deadwood was packed shoulder to shoulder with eager miners, merchants, hard-cases, and whores.

All had gotten the word and come out to witness the spectacle. The ultimate spectacle. A human being's staged death. Only this particular time, the big event would be multiplied by two.

Two men were slated to die this day, and there was an additional spice to the occasion, since the unfortunate pair were both hated Chinese.

Cries of "Filthy foreigners!" and "Savage heathen!" rose in the dusty air. The gulch that this town and diggings occupied was narrow and winding but fairly deep, and rock and mud faces played strange tricks with noise. Hoofbeats of horses being ridden to the center of the excitement sounded like distant thunder.

The yells of the souvenir hawkers echoed in all corners of the town: "Handbills, get your handbills! Only one thin nickel!" "Bits of a hangman's rope! Bloodied by the last victim! Cheap at the price!" And out-bawling them all: "Schooners of beer here! Toast the murderers' neck-stretch in suds. Only a quarter!"

And the folks were buying at the quadrupled price. Thirsty men weren't about to abandon a spot with a decent view. Not with the action about to begin any minute.

So far, however, all actual activity involving lawmen, the hangman, and the condemned culprits were concealed from public sight by the walls of the jailhouse. But within, things were happening rapidly during these last minutes before Chen and Fong got marched forth and were forced to mount the scaffold. The back room held a small crowd of its own, including, besides the comdemned men, Marshal Wilmer, a leggy, sour-faced preacher, and three armed deputies.

Zachariah Tree engaged himself with strict concentration, pinioning the second of the Chinamen's arms to his sides. The other stood to one side, already bound by the special four-inch leather waist strap and two-inch arm straps. Tree trussed the man's wrists together in front like his pard's, and then strapped together his knees.

The last walk outside would amount to an awkward shambling, but the straps prevented quick breaks for freedom. Fear didn't always make culprits feel helpless, Tree had learned, but often gave them strength beyond their size; strength powered by a kind of madness.

The hangman fastened the final buckle and straightened up from his crouch. He turned to Mike Wilmer grimly. "All set. I rigged the ropes and tied both noose knots earlier."

"I seen the gallows, Tree. Say one rope, it's longer than the other, you know that? A lot longer."

"This here culprit weighs less," Tree explained, pointing to Fong, the shorter Chinaman. "He gets a longer drop so's to break his neck. That other one can't take the long drop. His head might just pull off."

"Is this explanation essential?" complained the preacher, a trifle green faced.

"The prisoners don't know our lingo," Wilmer affirmed.

"I was referring to my own discomfort!"

Tree ignored the Bible thumper. So did the others. The hangman drew a neatly printed form from his black coat's side pocket. "Nothing's left but the work to be done outside. But first — "

"I got to sign your authorization to hang? Oh, all right!" As the marshal scribbled in a crabbed hand, Tree watched the culprits' faces. Fear was building in the pair. The hangman nodded, and the deputies moved.

Out under the sky, the crowd's hatred was a tangible thing. Such was often the way at hangings, but the feeling this time seemed to Tree extreme. The hate was out of proportion to the worth of Alonzo Jones, the culprits' victim. The roar from the spectators surrounding the scaffold was deafening.

"Hoist the slant-eye varmints high!" "Let's see the stinking rat-soup drinkers empty in their britches! Hang the sonsabitches! Hang the sonsabitches!"

Tree stood to full height, his black attire stark and striking. His new white shirt gleamed. Tree always wore a new or laundered shirt at every hanging out of respect for the unlucky ones set to meet their ends.

"Swing 'em," the crowd sang out now. "String up the damned devil slants!"

Since the two culprits couldn't speak English, Tree didn't ask them if they had any last words before he put the blindfolds on them. That accomplished, he yanked the trip lever and dropped the heavy traps without warning to the crowd.

The mob went wild.

The two men dropped like plummets, each to the end of his rope, then each suddenly jerked to a halt. The cannon-loud trap crash gave way to twin pops, like reports of small pistols. After the two Chinamen's necks snapped, they swung limp, twisting briskly in the air. Finally, the ropes' torque slowed. The waxy-skinned throats were stretched visibly.

The fronts and rears of the men's loose, baggy trousers became fouled. An acrid smell went up and floated around the scaffold.

"Hurray!" surged the great crowd noise. "Hurray! Hurray!"

The rank atmosphere of death failed to elate Zack Tree. The hangman felt far from triumphant. But that wasn't the case with the lawman Wilmer, happily shaking a grinning deputy's hand; the paste-faced parson's, too. Perhaps because the hanged men hadn't been Christian. By now those in the street around the tall, open platform were slapping handy backs. Tilted bottles drooled swigs of whiskey. Some miners strove to dance jigs. It was time for the hangman to make a quiet departure. The corpses would be left to swing for at least a long half hour. Such was insurance against the remote chance of revival. But Tree knew well that he'd been thorough in the performance of his duty. Justice done again, thought the man in black as he descended the steps. He felt his usual satisfaction at a job well done.

Trodding the ground beside the scaffold, again Tree made his difficult way as the people pushed and shoved about him on every side. Elbowing through the mass of well-wishers, though, he found himself suddenly confronted. The young woman in his path was angry as a cornered bobcat, judging by the expression on her pretty face. Her smooth, round cheeks were flushed darkly, and the dimpled chin thrust out.

"Zachariah Tree, I deplore you! You're a beast, and should be ashamed! There!"

He couldn't get past her, but neither could he retreat. At his back the crowd had closed, a seething mass of packed humanity. "I'd be obliged if you let me pass, ma'am. I'm in a rush."

"Not to hide your face, I'll warrant!" she cried. "Although that would be the only proper course!"

A shove from behind sent him bumping into her. The shapely form in the prim, high-necked dress flinched. The woman caromed into the gallows frame and recoiled. Now, with one hand steadying herself, she shook her honey-blond curls. "Don't you dare touch me! Killer!"

He had heard it before, many times. "Ma'am, I did my job, is all. We need hangmen in this world."

"Need, yes! To execute the wicked! And there are plenty of those! May they one day be rooted out, gone!"

"Then, lady, why — ?"

"Why am I angry, you contemptible man? I'm a willful gal, and I speak my mind! And you've plain done wrong this day! You just have to be told!"

"Told what, ma'am?"

"Ask around the diggings! Ask in China-town!" She thrust her face close once more, bright green eyes blazing. "Search inside your-self!"

# THE HANGMAN

He felt her sweet breath on his face. "Mr. Hangman, those two Chinese men today weren't guilty! You have hanged two poor, innocent souls by the neck!"

# Chapter Four

The hangman stood rooted for a moment under the shadow of the towering gallows. He had been struck hard by the short speech of the blond woman who now had vanished. Several foul-smelling drunk miners were pressing liquor on Tree, but he was in no mood for a drink and brushed them off.

Tree looked over at the slack corpses of the two Chinamen swaying in the dusty air. When he thought of his nooses biting into their stretched necks, his stout straps binding the stiffening limbs, Zachariah Tree felt strange. Until a minute or so ago, he had been certain of Chen and Fong's guilt. The case was open and shut. Brutal murderers tried and sentenced. A simple, straightforward execution performed.

Zachariah Tree was a man of conscience, and now his conscience pricked him.

He had never before hanged innocent men. He always took great care to review the case beforehand with the authorities and to talk with the culprits during the measuring. If the guilt were questionable, he would stall. Only when the affair was cleared and the slate cleaned would he proceed. He had often uncovered miscarriages of justice before it was too late. This procedure had saved dozens of wrongly accused people from hanging over the years and exposed the true criminals.

Zack Tree had taken all the right precautions in this case, as well. He had spoken with the judge and with the marshal, and both were satisfied as to the guilt of Chen and Fong. He couldn't talk with the culprits on account of their foreign lingo, but the evidence seemed clear. Now, a fine-looking female whose name he didn't know had accused him of killing innocent men.

And somehow, he felt she was telling the truth.

The town around him was too riotous with celebration over the deaths of the two Chinese for him to decide what to do next. Tree wanted out of Deadwood, clear out so he could think. He picked up his equipment from the marshal later, as he'd arranged. Up the dusty street he spied a crude sign: Livery Stable. There was a real barn there, if unpainted, and in the rear, a pole corral. He hiked in that direction, as fast as he could elbow through the eddying mob.

When he reached the place, the office was empty. No one was in sight. "Hello, in the back!" Tree shouted loudly. No response.

Tree strode around to the scruffy rear yard. There he found pack saddles, stock saddles, even an ancient Mcclellan propped on a rail. From there he could see the penned stock much better. They were a nondescript lot, but for a single close-coupled dove gray gelding. That one just might be worth riding, he speculated. He cast about for someone to discuss the animal with.

"Howdy," came a voice from off to the side. Tree swung to face the newcomer.

He was only a kid of sixteen or thereabouts, although his lean shoulders were packed with muscle over a broad and powerful chest. Under a buckskin vest, his only garment above the waist, the youth's skin was swarthy. Tree expected an accent, perhaps Mexican, but he was wrong. A row of white, straight teeth winked as the stable kid grinned and repeated his greeting. "My name's Dan, and I work here. How can I help you, mister?"

"I want to rent a horse," Tree said. "*That* one, to take a ride on." He pointed at the gray.

"Bring him back later today?"

"I reckon. My room's paid for at the Dakota House."

It didn't take more than a few minutes for the strapping youth to saddle the gray and bring him around. Tree paid the two-dollar fee and prepared to step into leather. "By the way," he got the notion to say first. "You happen to know a blond lady from these parts, maybe twenty-five, dresses plumb nice. Not the look of a tart?"

"Can't say as I do."

"Much obliged," Tree said, mounting the gray.

"Aiming to do another hanging, mister?"

The hangman looked down at the boy without answering and urged his horse forward.

Breaking from the aimless array of makeshift dwellings that ringed the boomtown within minutes, Tree rode the winding trail that led upslope into the rugged hills. All along the route, lean-tos and cabins clustered on claims, but the farther he traveled into the mountains, the more scattered they became. Most, even those perched on precarious ridges, seemed to be occupied. If men weren't actually working with picks or pans or sluice boxes, then one or more would be standing ready with rifles and shotguns to protect their claim from unwanted strangers. Scrambling after dust or nuggets was hard work, and finding pay dirt could lure a jumper's bullet.

Just ahead rose a looming outcrop in the shape of a huddled bear. Tree recalled it from a description given by the marshal. Just beyond, he'd been told, lay the disputed claim, the one sold to Chen and Fong by Jones. And there, too, was the hut where vigilante searchers had found the murder weapon.

He reined the gray horse off the trail and up the craggy slope toward the place.

First came the whine of the zinging bullet, then the vicious tug at the frock coat's sleeve. Finally the sharp, stick-snap crack of the rifle shot. Bushwhack! Zack Tree dove from the saddle, spooked the horse with a flying rump slap, and let it bolt away, all the while running for the concealment of a greasewood clump guarded by rocks. But the route was up a steep slope of loose shale, and his boots skidded dangerously.

More hot lead peppered the ground at the hangman's heels. A shrub he leaped past was blown from its roots and hurled to the dust. Tree reached the crest and went over it stumbling, falling flat but at least he was shielded. He rolled to his feet without losing momentum, and came up fisting his big Colt .44-40. He spun, waving the Peacemaker, and threw himself in against the ridge. He peeped quickly over it, and drew a spanging, shard-flinging round.

"Shit!" he spit out. He was pinned tight. Still, he was armed and had an entire shell belt full of spare bullets. Thumbing open the six-gun's loading gate, he shoved a sixth cartridge into the chamber that he normally kept empty for safety.

Spying a gentle incline sweeping to his left, Tree saw his chance to climb above the bushwackers. His hunch was strong that the shots had come from the Chinamen's claim. Only, why somebody was defending it seemed a puzzle right now.

Tree climbed and sweated through a corridor cleft of stone, then a dry water course, and finally atop a ridge. From the high vantage point he

31

scanned the gulch below, and saw a creek trickling in a sandy bed, drab gray granite faces, and a hut. As he had been told, it was no more than a roof of sticks suspended on piled stones. Snakes and scorpions would have free access. One hell of a spot to live, he thought. Most wouldn't even call it living. Chen and Fong called it home.

Peering cautiously from cover, Zachariah Tree now saw a lone gunman for the first time. From the fifty-or-so yard distance, the weapon appeared to be a battered Henry carbine. The face under the slouch hat was beard-stubbled and moan. He knew he'd have to kill the hardcase, but he hoped he could get some answers from him first.

Tree began with care to make his way over the ridge and along the slope's face to close distance. A good many minutes had passed, but at last he crouched tense and ready right above the jasper. The idea was to get the jump on him within pistol range and force him to talk.

Tree bunched his leg muscles and launched into space. He landed catfooted, but by chance the hardcase turned, then cursed and threw his long gun to his shoulder in a fluid move. Tree dove, and swung his big Colt like a club to knock the rifle's barrel aside as the thing went off. He felt the heat of the muzzle blast as the roar battered his ears, but he had managed to tackle the man and hurl him backward.

He slammed against a boulder, and Tree was on him again, this time driving his left fist to the jutting jaw. The gent retaliated with the hands that he had freed by dropping his weapon. Grabbing Tree's lapels, he jerked him within range, then pumped a knee to his groin. Pain shot through his lower body as if he had been speared. The hangman reeled and doubled over.

A blow to his kidneys propelled Tree from his feet. He looked up, saw his enemy about to drop on him, and kicked out hard and quickly. The toe of his heavy stovepipe boot slammed into the attacker's chest. At the same time, the man in black crawfished, then came around powerfully with a tight blow to stun his opponent. He climbed to his feet, dragging the jasper after.

"I don't take kindly to tossed bullets," Tree said, "and that one near parted my hair. You better talk fast. Who in hell are you? What you doing on this here claim?"

"No, my pard don't got to talk," rasped a harsh voice. Tree tensed. Another jasper stood behind him. The hangman heard a shotgun's ominous click. "Now you take them hands off Mel, else I ventilate you." Tree believed the man.

The fellow had crept near while Tree was dusting up the pard. "All right, you two boys got me. I won't be making no move," Tree casually lied. "Still, a man wonders what you're doing here on mining property where you got no business."

Tree, now facing both Shotgun and the other hardcase, gauged his chances. By putting the brawny but unarmed one as a human shield, he could likely keep Shotgun from going off. It seemed his best bet, at least. Better than letting his head be blown off. But the claim jumpers, if that's what they were, didn't seem so trigger-happy as before, but more inclined to perhaps trade words. "We got the right to be here," muttered the one who had held the rifle.

"The Chinese that worked the claim, they're dead."

"We got the right to be here."

"Can't say I represent Chen and Fong, exactly, but — "

"You'd best be on your way, mister!"

Tree scowled. "Maybe I'd come back with Marshal Wilmer."

"Makes no never mind. Y'see — "

"No!" Tree spun on his heel, stooped to retrieve his dropped six-gun, and jammed it, uncocked, into his holster. "I'll be leaving you boys alone for now. But don't figure that this thing is over!"

His neck crawled as he strode down the slope, but the hardcases didn't open fire. When he reached the grazing livery horse he mounted leisurely and kicked up into a trot.

In a minute Tree was threading the trail he'd come up.

On his ride back to Deadwood, the hangman was keenly aware of things that later could be important: the general lay of the land, the gulch, the locations of the various claims and which looked richer, which poorer. The way the prospecting game went, two sunken shafts merely a few yards apart might produce far different yields in pay dirt. He had been told that some of the miners along the stretch were striking it rich, digging hundreds of dollars' worth of nuggets daily, while others were starving. As he rode he was curious, too, about Chen and Fong's countrymen. They were supposed to be over-running the territory and robbing the earth of the wealth white men believed was theirs. But as yet, Tree had seen no Chinese miners or pro-spectors.

But now he spotted a thin column of smoke rising above the nearby hills. One or more camp-fires must mean some mining activity — claims. The hangman resolved on an inspection, and reined the gray up a rugged gap barely wide enough for the animal. With the hangman's stir-rups scraping boulders to either side, horse and rider made their way.

They emerged finally onto a flat, and into the midst of a modest diggings area. And each of the staked claims was being toiled on by scamper-ing, chattering — Chinese!

But the rapid talk in the foreign tongue stopped as if by spigot when the men noticed Tree. The small yellow-skinned men —there were no females to be seen — all stood frozen, holding their tools and staring at the new arriv-al.

"Howdy," Tree called out. "Likely nobody here knows me, and you got a right to be suspicious, but I do mean well." Tree gently urged the geld-ing forward. A couple of your people, Chen and Fong, well, they were hanged today in town. I been wondering about next of kin — that is, this side of the China Sea. Anybody here know who mighten inherit? There's a gold claim, likely worthless, but still — "

None among the Chinese moved or spoke.

"Folks, I said . . ." But it was becoming clear that even if they could understand, they viewed him with distrust.

He scanned the round, uplifted faces again, and found them all mere impassive, blank masks.

Realizing he'd best look for information elsewhere, Tree turned the horse, kicked it to a trot, and headed back the way that he had come.

The Chinese didn't go back to work until he was swallowed by the deep, steep draw.

36

# Chapter Five

"Damn it, Enos, why'd you let on the case was cut and dried? Now it turns out that Chen and Fong denied they were guilty!" Zack Tree stood over Enos Depew's form, huddled in the rocker, and practically shouted at the scrawny, slouched judge.

The judge's face, wreathed in seams and wrinkles, had gone chalk-pale. His forehead carried a sheen of sweat, and the shock of snowy hair was damp, as well.

"No cause for shouting, son. Let's have us a drink and . . ."

Tree rolled his eyes to the magistrate's shake ceiling. "Shit, you look like you had your share already. Were you drunk when you sat on the bench at those Chinamen's trial, too, Enos?"

37

Depew worked his mouth without speaking. Tree turned on his heel and paced. Beyond the clouded window glass the day was far from over, but his hopes just about were. Hopes of getting the revealing facts he wanted out of this miserable excuse for a man.

He'd seen it before in other men: the harsh effects of too much cheap liquor on the system of a person. Even a person one might otherwise respect. Last evening there had been the smell of whiskey about Enos Depew, true, but his friend had always been a drinking man. But the magistrate was beyond mild intoxication. His eyes were bloodshot and watering, and his liver-spotted hands lay in his lap, trembling. Disgusted, Tree strode to the tall china press standing empty-shelved against the wall. He pulled the lower doors open with a jerk. There it was, the nearly drained quart bottle that bore no label.

"Depew, when I'd heard tell that your wife died sudden and you'd been through some bad times, I figured you'd up and retire. But then I got your telegram and was right proud that you were the kind of man didn't let life get you down. Now, it appears you ran a trial when you oughtn't to have, and a couple of men charged with murder didn't get them a fair chance at justice. And I might've hung two innocent men!"

He hurled the bottle to crash against the wall next to which Depew sat. There was no reaction. The old man stared into space. "Well, I've said enough to you, old man. Maybe sometime your conscience will prick you like it should."

Tree strode out the door. The air smelled better under the high sky, but there remained a bad taste in the hangman's mouth. He swung into the gray's saddle and reined toward the main street.

The goings-on inside the jailhouse, specifically around the marshal's desk, didn't please Tree much when he walked in. But then, it was exactly what he might have expected. Two of the hulking part-time deputies employed by Wilmer were sprawled in chairs. The chief tin-star of the tribe had gone to the corner gun cabinet to fetch yet another bottle of forty-rod. He plunged the glass neck into his mouth, vised the cork between gapped teeth, and popped it. The potent amber liquid splashed his chin and the checked shirt he wore, but the accident produced only a raucous laughter. But the laughter stopped when the marshal spotted the hangman.

"Look, boys, it's the famous 'Hanging' Tree, none other! By God, Tree, you're welcome! Welcome as boiled rice to a chopstick toter!" A pause. "Hey, you ain't smiling!"

"Today Chinaman jokes ain't funny, Wilmer. I came over so's to have some words with you, but I see you're busy."

"Me'n the fellers, we been a-celebrating, Tree. If you got other ideas besides getting pissing drunk tonight, maybe you ain't so welcome after all." A hacking bout of coughs racked him. Tree could see he was skunk-squiffy and drooling, as were his sidekicks. Shards from a broken jug heaped messily in a corner. The man's breath reeked. "Well, hangman, what d'you want, if it ain't no swig o' squeezings?"

"I come to get my equipment. But first, I got a few questions about the killing of Alonzo Jones. Like who found the murdered jasper's body and the knife out at Chinamen's hut?"

Wilmer held the bottle tipped high to his puckered lips. His Adam's apple performed an imitation of a jumping frog. When he stopped, he stuck out his two chins and snarled: "Pears, mister, you got your complaints 'bout Deadwood law. Th' coolies is buried under a rock pile to-night. Not deep — let the coyotes fill their bellies. *You* don't like it, hangman, it's plumb sad, but — " he gave a tipsy leer, and shrugged — "hanging gear's out back."

"I asked some questions. And you can go to hell."

The fat lawman took another swig of rotgut and stood quickly. Then his face went from an alcohol-flushed red to ash gray. His knees buckled and he staggered back against the desk. Wilmer grabbed air and fell on his ass, then rolled over on the packed-dirt floor, out cold.

"Guess ol' Mike had enough. Right, boys?" one deputy said. The others laughed.

Tree moved close to the deputy and poked his finger into his chest. "You can tell your boss when he sleeps it off that I aim to get my own answers about the Jones killing — with or without his help." He stalked back out of the jail-house, collected his gear, and left.

Once back in the street, he turned the opposite way from the gallows, empty of bodies but still a dismal reminder of the work he had ahead of him. He walked to his boardinghouse to leave off his five-strand ropes and leather harnesses in his room, then headed out to find a saloon. It was as good a place to start looking for information as any.

The saloon he selected wasn't the fanciest in the row, but still it had one interesting touch. This was a false front, although the roof was no more than a canvas tarp. Inside, it was fairly bright, and plenty of sawdust had been spread on the floor. There was a a crude stage, but no performers at that early hour. The gamblers were hunched over their cards at tables in the back. Tree ambled to the pine plank that was the bar and bellied up among the drinkers. Some men looked like they'd had been there ever since the hanging and still interested in jawing about it.

One loud talker believed the execution was about the best he'd ever seen, on account it had two victims. The next man up the line agreed, but also pointed out that it had disposed of two hated yellow-skinned heathen. A huge barrel of a fellow with a scruffy beard allowed it was better than a circus he'd once seen in Dodge. Tree tried to ignore the surrounding voices and catch the attention of a barkeep. The small red-bearded man finally came over with a dirty, wet rag and a bottle of rye.

"I'll just have me a glass of what you're holding."

"Sure thing, mister. . . . Hey, ain't you the hangman?" the bar dog asked.

Tree nodded.

"Well, then, the first drink's on the house!"

The aproned man splashed the whiskey into a glass, then turned to go, when Tree grabbed his arm. "Much obliged, barkeep, but I'm looking for something to go with that drink."

"Ain't got no free lunch today."

"No, I'm looking for a lady."

"Ain't that many ladies in the camp. What'd she look like? Pretty?"

"I'd say so, yeah. Yellow hair, not tall."

The barman's attention was mainly on the loud argument breaking out at the end of the bar. "Had to've been Beaver Tooth Annabelle. Works a crib upstairs at the Nugget. Look out for that one, mister. She's been knowed to lift a man's poke if given the chance."

"I don't guess the lady I'm hunting is a — " Tree broke off because his listener had taken his leave, gone to settle the fracas by means of a swung bung starter.

Tree shrugged. The woman he sought wasn't the whore Beaver Tooth Annabelle. She had the look of a schoolmarm or a church lady.

He finished his drink and walked outside. By now he was thinking on another tack, and he angled across the rutted street toward a small building with a big sign stating: CLAIMS OFFICE.

His boots clattered on the step and on the poorly nailed floorboards inside. There, he was peered at by a scarecrow-thin fellow in dark sleeve protectors, standing at a file drawer. The claims recorder casually cocked an eyebrow.

"Well, any later in the day and I couldn't have helped you, mister. But there's still a few minutes before closing. You want to file a claim? Take a chair, and I'll get the papers."

Tree set the man straight. "I didn't drop by to file a claim. My name's Tree, and I've come for some information on a claim that's been owned by some other folks. You'll likely know which claim when I tell you it figured in a murder trial. Chen and Fong. That's the pair that was hanged today."

"Claims material is held confidential, mister. Any special reason you want to know?"

"You could say I got a special interest in the case, Mr . . ."

"Donleavy. Alfred Donleavy." He curled his lips, then went on. "I can't show you no records without a writ from the court."

Tree looked hard at the clerk.

"Uh . . . well, I reckon since you're the hangman, hired by the judge, that makes you an officer of the court. 'Sides, them Chinamen won't mind nohow. Wait here."

It took less than a minute. Alfred Donleavy pored first in a cupboard and then in a drawer of an ancient desk. The material he plopped down on the desk top consisted of a book — a very large book — and a sheet of printed paper that bore a few handwritten lines. "There you be," the small man said. "Now let me stay clean out of your way. . . ." The official busied himself, turning back to his stacks and stacks of file drawers. Tree scanned the page that the book lay open to.

All of a sudden, the hangman's task didn't seem so easy. A quick glance at the columns of names revealed no Chen, no Fong, and no Alonzo Jones. The puzzle was only compounded when Tree compared the name on the one separate sheet. There, the owner of the described claim was filled in as one Samuel Griswold. Although the name wasn't exactly unfamiliar, Tree didn't see quite how it fit here. He motioned to Donleavy, and the recorder strolled over.

"I asked about the claim of the dead Chinese fellers?"

"That's it in front of you. That's its description on the sheet."

"But the name — ?"

Donleavy heaved an impatient sigh. "Mr. Tree, the book lists the transactions in the order that they're made. That includes all filings and all transfers made in case of sale. And, according to the record, there was no transfer of the property in question. That claim never officially changed hands."

Tree rubbed his chin with his palm. "Is that fact?"

"It's all in the record book. This Griswold feller filed back in March, which, by the way, was before *I* came to these here parts."

"Where does Alonzo Jones fit in then?"

The little man shrugged. "All I know is, a few weeks ago there was talk all over the camp about his murder. Then the Chinamen were caught and jailed, and the marshal showed a bill of sale. Evidence. The trial was quick, over in an hour, and the jury — miners all — they found for guilty."

"How could Jones sell if he didn't own the claim?"

Another shrug. "Nobody raised the question. There was the bill of sale, if no real transfer of a deed. I didn't go to watch the trial myself. Just read about it in the *Clarion*."

Tree looked up suspiciously. "No one asked you to check the claim?"

"For a couple yellow-hides charged with killing a white man? That's what the heathen do, skulk around with wicked knives they use. Be a good thing when they're all dead, else cleared out of the country. The government never should've — "

Tree stood up and tugged his hat a trifle lower over his brow. "Well then, Donleavy, thanks for your help. Reckon I'll be moseying. It's getting late."

"Yeah, that's c'rect, sir. Got my wife and the babe waiting to home, and I never do get enough time with them. Glad to've been of help to you."

As Tree shut the door to the office, Donleavy turned the OPEN sign to CLOSED and doused the lamplight.

"Damn," the hangman muttered, again shuffling through flour-fine street dust underfoot. He rounded the wall of the half-tent on the corner and collided with a pretty female. At her side walked a barefoot boy of ten or twelve. The woman drew back, grabbing at her dislodged little hat.

"Sorry, ma'am."

"Mister, you ought to learn to watch your step — "

The two both froze at the same instant, eyes staring; one pair iron gray, the other green. Why, you — "

It was the same woman who had challenged Tree that morning beside the gallows. Now the hangman blurted quickly, "Lady, I've been looking for you."

"Have you, Mr. Tree? Well, it appears you've found me. But I haven't time for you at the moment. Jory here's just come on the run. There's an emergency back at my office. So, if you'll only let me pass — "

She swept past with a flounce of her serge skirts. "Lady, you said some things before. . . ."

Now the woman and kid were actually running. They veered around the corner of the blacksmith's and up a narrow side street. Up ahead, as Tree kept pace, a small gang of men came into view. By their mud-stained, scroungy look, Zack could tell the noisy bunch were miners.

They milled and grumbled in front of another new, unpainted slab structure. Over the door was an ornately lettered sign: THE DEADWOOD CLARION.

As the trio hurried up, a tall, sandy-haired man was being dragged from the doorstep. A barrel-chested mob member punched the mild and handsome face. "Take that, you heathen-lovin' scum!"

"Phil!" screeched the woman just ahead of Tree, lurching forward and swinging her own small fist.

"Well, damned if it ain't the bitch!" snarled the unshaven mob leader. "Grab her, too, boys! Do her rough, if you've got a mind!"

A dirty, hammy hand clutched the woman's arm. The kid rushed in, only to be knocked aside like a stem of dry grass.

"Hey!" Tree yelled. "Can't the fracas be parlayed? Ain't no call to treat a woman like a — "

A horde of drunken, hate-crazed eyes locked on the hangman. "Feller's buyin' in! *Get* the son of a bitch!"

The gang of roughnecks charged.

# Chapter Six

Zack Tree's eyes darted over to the area where the newspaper office stood. There was the building itself, on which the hangman noted a broken windowpane and the tiny yard, towered over by a pin oak. The angry group of men from the town advanced with bunched fists and more than a few clubbed boards and wheel spokes.

Off at the margin of Tree's vision, the sandy-haired man was still taking hard punishment. And directly in front of the hangman the woman fought the bruiser who was pinning her arm. She struck him across the nose with her reticule, and he swore a string of oaths.

Enough was enough.

Tree's hand flew to the holster at his belt, and came up, lightning-fast, with his cocked and leveled Colt. "Hold on!" the hangman snapped. The wall of men stopped as if invisibly leashed. "Hoist your hands! Let the gal and Phil, there, go!" The jaspers obeyed the hangman grudgingly, but if looks could kill, Tree would have been dead as a maggot-swarmed dog.

"Mr. Tree, watch out!"

The hangman whirled at the woman's shouted warning, and saw the lone miner, his Bowie drawn, darting low and close for a quick sneak slash. He brought the .44 around in a smooth motion and fired. The man dropped the knife and grabbed his bleeding arm.

"Anybody else?" Nobody spoke. Nobody moved.

Tree stood in a poised crouch, the six-gun now recocked and ready in his steady fist. Seconds dragged past under the purpling sunset sky, and the man in black sensed the miners' resolve going up in smoke. It was time to put an end to the confrontation. "The way I see it, fellers, you got a choice: clear out or eat lead."

Grumbling, the group started eroding from the back, by pairs and threes, drifting away out of the big oak's gloomy shadow. Then the main body of miners broke up all at once, the leader helping the wounded man as he staggered off, and glaring at Tree and his companions over a slouched shoulder.

"There," he declared when once alone with the woman and the sandy-haired man. He didn't need to tell the pair that they were lucky. It was written in their faces that they understood.

"Well, then, Phil, are you all right?" The blonde was smoothing her blouse and the wrinkled skirt below it. A good deal of the pale hair had slipped from its bun to string downward in soft tendrils.

"I'll survive, Becky," Phil said, turning toward Tree. "Mister, we owe you our thanks today, and that's the plain truth. Those men were plenty riled." He offered his hand. "I'm Phil Dunmore. I run the paper. And this is my wife, Rebecca. Didn't see where young Jory ran off to. He's our junior jack of all trades."

"The kid lit a shuck off back to the main street," Tree said. "Don't reckon I blame him. He got him a powerful scare."

"Didn't we all?" Dunmore said. "Becky, I don't know as I'm acquainted with the friend you brought."

"He isn't a friend, exactly, Phil." She tossed her curls. "Husband of mine, meet Zachariah Tree."

The newspaperman's expression fell. He slowly wiped his hands on the ink-stained apron that he wore, and went on as if lost in thought. "Tree. Tree the hangman. It's funny in a way, your turning up and saving our bacon. Those miners wouldn't have been stirred up and come over here but for today's lead item in the *Clarion*. And, of course, the famous hangman figures in the story."

Phil Dunmore took out a folded sheet of newsprint from his apron and handed it to the man in black. Tree's eyes fell immediately on the piece in question; it ran center column in bold type, and related details of the execution of the two Chinese. From the first line there was no doubt that the writer was opposed. The hangings were deemed outrageous, the man in charge called a brute allowed to kill with legal sanction.

"Hard stuff," Tree said, looking up, meeting Rebecca Dunmore's round blue eyes. "I can see why the town might be riled. It reads here as how the jurymen were plumb fools to have convicted those men."

"I wrote the truth as I saw it," the woman stated flatly. "I attended the trial in that disgusting old saloon. Everyone hates Chinese people so much, evidence didn't seem to matter. The guilty verdict was assured from the start."

Tree considered for a moment, then said, "Somebody did knife Alonzo Jones to death. If the accused didn't commit the murder, who did? And why?"

"Common robbers?" the husband questioned.

In the fading dusk, the hangman peered at him. "Maybe. But here's a different notion in my head. If Jones had him another enemy, or was up to his ears in some kind of plot, that could be the reason he died.'

Rebecca and Phil Dunmore looked puzzled. "Tree," Phil said, "we know that the trial was a pretext and a farce, but that's all we can be sure of. You're sounding less like a hangman by the minute, and more like a decent human with a healthy curiosity. But the idea of some sort of plot involving Jones seems farfetched."

Tree scratched his chin. "Did you know Jones never even owned that claim he'd lived on?"

The couple exchanged glances.

"Mr. Tree, it's gotten dark outside, the air's full of mosquitoes, and you keep surprising us with your tidbits of information. Could be it's time we all sat down, got comfortable, and talked it all out. Let's step inside, why don't we? Becky will light a lamp, and we can carry this on over a good, hot supper."

Sitting down at a rickety table in the printing office, Tree could see that the newspaper still had a long way to go before it made money for its owners. However, the Dunmores insisted on sharing supper with their guest, and made him welcome in the corner that served as a kitchen. Tree watched Rebecca bustle at the ancient cookstove, enjoying the woman's sleek looks and her graceful way of moving.

As the talk changed to less serious matters just before the meal, he studied on the couple's manner of speech. It was eastern for sure, and Tree pegged both host and hostess as New Englanders. He'd met some Yankee prisoners from those parts back during the War Between the States, and in fact had them under his charge for a spell. But when Grant's army had moved south, Lee had fallen back, and the whole situation dissolved into the Confederacy's pitiful last gasp. Six weeks later, the young Texan was back home in his native Trinity River country. The times had been crazy then, but they were crazy now, too, Tree knew. It was something that seemed constant across every span of years: folks' greed and selfishness.

The woman dished up the meal, consisting of warmed-over stew with fresh biscuits and a few greens, and they all pitched in around a battered deal table. Although the man's civility remained, prompted by gratitude, the woman was cool, still far from completely melted. Feeding a hangman was obviously a new experience.

"We brought the old Excelsior press and type fonts over the prairie in a mule-drawn wagon," Phil Dunmore related as he plied his fork. "Got us set up under the spreading oak you saw, Tree, and put out our first Deadwood edition two days after we arrived."

"How long you been in Deadwood, Dunmore?"

"Less than six months. It was rough getting through the winter, but then circulation began to pick up. We like to think it happened because of our quality, but the other local sheet did fold about that time."

Rebecca Dunmore rose and fetched the coffeepot. "More coffee?" Phil asked. She splashed dark liquid in Zack Tree's cup and set the pot in the center of the table. "Mr. Tree, let's talk more on the reason you're here. Alonzo Jones's murder. You declared a few minutes ago that the man didn't own the claim. That would suggest that he salted it, sold it, pocketed the money — but the real owner never stepped in? I don't see as that's too likely."

"Claims-office records read that a man named Griswold staked it out, and the property never changed hands. Samuel Griswold — ever hear of the feller?"

"Yes, Phil and I have heard of Griswold. He's one of the richest men here in town. Various business interests, mostly unsavory."

"A house of ill fame, he runs," the husband put in. "I've heard that Griswold lived in Denver before the Black Hills rush. It may or may not be true. He's not the kind, I'd think, to let himself be cheated."

"Can you tell me any more?"

"I can't imagine what it would be."

"Then we got us a mystery, it appears." Tree finished his coffee and set down the cup. "Well, I'd best be going. Didn't aim to keep you folks up so late." The hangman rose, plucked his black frock coat from the chairback, and shrugged into it. "Ma'am, thanks for the tasty eating." The woman could write news stories with more flavor than her food, Tree thought, however.

"If I interpret you correctly, Tree," Phil Dunmore added, "you're not going to let this Jones thing drop. But what does it all matter to you at this late date? As a hangman, you did your job, and presumably got your pay."

"Oh, I always get my coin in advance, all right," the man in black confessed. "What's my interest anymore, then? It's true enough I can't bring Chen and Fong back. But, folks, it's more than just me feeling foolish about my rep for always doing executions right and proper. This one time I got told about the case by someone as let me down. Somewhere out there a killer is on the loose who went to some trouble to load blame on two innocent Chinamen. I don't cotton to him getting away scot free."

At the door the couple watched as the hangman made his way along the path that would return him to the town's busy center. Clouds scudded across the night sky to screen the moon, and Tree's form moved in a ghostly silver glow.

"So the hangman turns out a more decent person than I'd thought," the newspaperman mused aloud. "You were on edge while he was in the room, Becky, but I felt we owed him civility, seeing that he drove away those troublemakers." He circled her waist with his arm.

Despite the warmness of the night air, her skin wore goose bumps. "I can't forget the job he does, Phil. Oh, he was on his good behavior, true, but a man like that, who's killed scores and scores — " Abruptly she broke off and drew her husband back inside. "I can't help the way I feel," the woman added. "The man gives me the shivers."

The pair moved together toward the building's darkened rear. And then the last light was snuffed out.

The door slammed open into the drab crib above the Elephant Saloon, and the big man and the pasty, flab-fleshed woman staggered across the threshold. The stark coal-oil lamplight revealed dingy walls, a cracked washbasin, and a rusty bed adorned with splotched and rumpled sheets. In the center of the floor, "Bull Shoulders" yanked his companion to a halt, and bent abruptly to kiss the smeared carmine lips. Her hand found his groin and massaged roughly for a minute. Then he broke the embrace, hoisted, and dropped the hefty female on the mattress.

There was the creak of metal joints as he climbed aboard, too, following sounds of tearing cloth and gusted sighs. With the front of his baggy trousers torn open, he mounted her. Mud-caked boots dug straw tick violently. Callused fingers tweaked bared nipples the size of pancakes. "Ah, Paddy boy! Ahh, *ah*!

"Say it, gal! Tell me what I like to hear!"

"You're the biggest, greatest . . . *Irishman* that be! . . . Carryin' the biggest, greatest — " Her last words were lost in a flurry of furious, pleasure-racked shrieks.

The pair subsided slowly, their sweat drying on them. A draft of night breeze from the tiny window cooled the damp, sun-roughened brows. After a long time, the woman began to twitch to the music filtering up from the barroom below: an out-of-tune piano, a fractured soprano. Paddy's hamlike paw groped beneath the bed. . . .

"Shit! Piss!"

"Sure, and what's the matter, darlin'?"

"Went for me whiskey bottle stashed 'neith the bed. Stuck a hand in the thunder mug! God-damned mess!"

She thrust her bosom at his long-jawed face, but his irritation failed to melt. "Saints preserve us, but the hand stings fearsome! The one I hurt, trying to bust the skull of the bloody newspaperman."

"The *Clarion*'s owner, who condemned all you jurymen."

"C'rect! As if the Chinese rat eaters are men, and it matters that a pair got their necks stretched. I tell you, me gal — "

"What you ain't told me yet, Paddy, nor anyone downstairs, neither, is what happened over there today. You said you tried to bust his head. I can't believe the chappie fought you off, him and that slip of a wife." The woman smirked.

"There was another fellow stuck his nose in," the Irishman growled. He pulled a gun. Shot Lucky Jack Blair in the wing, which I guess tells you what's in a name. The rest of our crew turned tail. I couldn't go the gunman alone."

The rummaging man had found the spirits bottle, and he immediately thrust it to his mouth. He drank for ten full seconds with his Adam's apple bobbing like a fisherman's cork. He finished with a noisy smack and threw it against the wall.

The woman had slipped from the bed and stood teetering, barely covered by her rumpled clothes. The loose skin on her arms shone the color and consistency of dough. And as she'd watched the man, her bloodshot eyes widened in fear.

The fear was justified. Rage turned the man's features beet red and he hurled the bottle to smash against the wall. "Paddy Riley," she blurted, "now you've — "

His bloated face swung toward her. Leaping from the mattress, he buried a bunched fist to the woman's middle. "Huh! Take you this, Nell Conway! Ya'll not smirk nor laugh no more at Paddy!" He struck her again, this time backhand across the cheek. Her lip split and the cut sprayed blood. He pumped a kick to her side, and she fell with a crash.

"Damn you, Paddy! Damn you!" she said as she lay in a huddled lump in the corner.

"Well, I learned one thing from ye! Revenge feels fine! Damned fine, by the saints! Now, listen, woman, and listen good! I'll have that man's hide!"

He jerked her head back by the hair. Blood trickled where she'd lost a tooth.

"I'll slit his gizzard, d'ye hear?"

"I h-hear, Paddy."

He was tugging up his filthy twill trousers. "So, maybe I'll fetch ye his lopped-off ear!"

And then the big man with the charming brogue was gone. She was alone with her few possessions in the world, her hurt, and her thoughts.

# Chapter Seven

It was midnight and the old-timer at the saloon bar with Tree was drunk and talkative.

He'd been building to reach this state for hours, since well before the hangman found him, two drinking establishments ago. The men had moved together from the Parrot's Perch to the Alamo, and now the pair trod the sawdust at the Crystal Pistol, one of Deadwood's rowdiest. All around Tree and Uncle Billy Huckadoo, the noise in the large barroom roared. The patrons beehiving the place whooped and shouted. On a small stage across the floor, a line of four young women moved to music. Long net-stockinged legs kicked high and flashed and pranced.

But it all formed the background for Zachariah Tree's serious business, which was working on Uncle Billy. They'd covered the gray-beard's mountain-man life back before the war, and the buffalo hunting-days way down in Kansas. But for five years now, Uncle Billy had been a prospector, and although he'd never made a big strike, he had survived and become an expert in the way of miners' lore.

"Helena, up Montana way," the old-timer cackled, "now there was a boomtown in its day." A frown crossed his saddle brown face. "Gettin' peaceful lately. Got 'em a schoolhouse now, and a big new church!"

"Billy, it appears you been all over."

"But never east of the Mississippi, hangman. Never east of the old Mississip!"

"A matter of pride with you?"

"Betcha!" Laughter croaked in the skinny neck.

Tree splashed more Old Overholt in their glasses. "Getting back to what you said before, Billy, about salting claims . . ."

"Got that on your brain, have ya?"

"More or less. Seems the best way to do it is with a gun? Just curious, mind."

A sly wink. "Oh, sure. Sure. Though lots of the boys have favored the gold-salts-tonic way. Gold salts — the medicine for kidney complaint? Drink the stuff, piss on the ground, it can lift an assay, not much, but sometimes enough."

Tree made a show of looking at his nickel-plated Waterbury fob watch. "Still, what interests me, old-timer, is the way with the gun. It ain't too late yet. You said awhile ago you'd be willing to show me."

"Hell, it's comfortable in here. Gonna be rainin' out there. Can feel it in my bones."

"There's a bottle in it for you."

Uncle Billy stretched and creaked up on bowed legs. "Son, them words do put life back in rheumatismed limbs!"

Tree had noticed from the beginning that all Deadwood was jammed into hollows between steep hills. The town had grown up helter-skelter, spreading from the main gulch into many crooked tributaries. Now treading the slope that the saloon row backed on, he was careful of his footing. Uncle Billy, though, for all his complaints, scrambled over rocks and boulders like a goat.

"How much farther to the place you picked?"

"Soon, hangman, soon now."

When the pair stood in a hollow surrounded by jagged, jumbled granite chunks, the oldster rooted in a pocket for a candle end.

"Spot'll do as good as any."

A lucifer match flared, and the old man lit the candle. There was no wind at all, and lightning flickered over distant mountain peaks.

"My old cap-and-ball Walker Colt happens to have a nice flare to the barrel. If a feller's got him no scatter gun, this kind of firearm'll do right fine." Tree watched closely as Billy fiddled with the weapon. "I got that gold dust right here that you give me a bit ago, hangman. O' course, coin filings'd work, too. See how I'm packin' the cylinder above the gunpowder? Easier than hell. Now there's a rock face over there we might try."

Without more folderol, he eared back the hammer, pointed the old primed pistol, and blazed away. When the echoing report died and the smoke cleared, the men strode to the targeted flat.

"There you be, hangman, now you see for yourself. The flaked gold sticks to the outside of the rocks, and 'pears powerful natural. A greenhorn comes this way, he might buy off the salter, but he'd be throwing cash away. Ain't no real ore underground here. What he'd think he saw's really just a show."

"A gold find that's nothing but a fake."

"It's what I said. Now about that bottle you give your word about — "

"Another question." As the candle flickered, Tree thrust his face near the prospector's. "Over the years, must be hundreds of suckers buying salted claims. How many do you reckon brought in the law with success? Charged the crooked sellers with fraud?"

"Why, none. With metal-minin' property, it's always been 'buyer, watch your ass.' 'Cept if the sellin' feller don't really own the claim."

Tree's interest leaped. "Selling a claim you don't own, that's against the law?"

"C'rect! A judge'll rule agin the cheater every time. Get the sucker's money back for him. If 'tain't spent, o' course."

Tree was standing, looking thoughtful.

"Say, Mr. Hangman, can't you feel the drizzles startin'? Don't want to be out here in the wet, gettin' caught in flash floods, whatever.'Bout that bottle of crack skull, now, I'll never be readier — "

"Uhuh." Tree grinned.

"You want to salt another face, I'm willin' to salt another face, b' God!"

"Well, Uncle Billy," Tree said, "I reckon I seen enough. And it is raining in the mountains, and just could blow this way — "

"You don't wanta hike all the way to a saloon with me? Well, this old coon'll take hard cash."

Tree tossed Billy a silver dollar and said a quick good-night.

Daylight that wasn't particularly brilliant slanted through the hotel window and across Tree's rented bed. The hangman popped open his eyes when he heard the knock at his door. He tried to ignore it, but it kept getting louder. Tree greeted the brand-new day. But a new day didn't always mean a fresh beginning, old feuds and fears banished. Taking no chances, he drew his Colt from the holster at the bed's head with his right hand.

He already clutched the Hopkins and Allen Captain Jack boot gun from under his pillow in his left hand.

"Who's out there?" the hangman called.

"Me!"

"Who in hell is 'me'?" The man in long johns threw the quilt aside and dropped his feet to the cool, smooth boards.

"Undertaker Nathan Bosley. Marshal Wilmer forgot to take all the gear, so I've fetched over your — "

Tree flipped the latch, tugged the handle, and the panel opened. "Toss them on the floor. You'll excuse it, if I don't invite you in."

"Fine by me, Mr. Tree. Just doing my job."

"And I'm much obliged to you, Bosley. Now I got to bid you a fast good day.'" He slammed the door in the man's long face.

"Son of a bitch. Up late last night, and now this." Tree slumped and viewed what had been delivered: a bundle of leather hand straps. All were neatly coiled, and showed the effects of fresh saddle soaping — spot cleaned, thoughtfully. But the gear reminded him of Fong and Chen, and he scowled at his reflection in the mirror.

He laid the six-guns on the commode and scooped up the straps. Next he padded to the wardrobe that held the leather traveling bag. Open, the bag displayed its contents, one side stuffed with fresh clothes and possibles. On the other side were closely packed hangman's supplies.

There were the coils of rope, five-strand hemp he'd used for Chen and Fong, four-ply for women, made specially for him by inmates in a Kansas prison. The wide leather body harnesses, a few more hand straps, and a supply of grooved rings of hammered brass.

Tree had invented those rings years before to avoid noose-knot slippage. Now, the problem was solved. He'd rotate the rings for every culprit. Private superstition kept him from using the same ring twice in a row.

Into the bag Tree now laid the straps the undertaker had returned, and then pulled forth a clean green shirt. He buckled the case up and turned again to the wall mirror.

Until springing the trapdoors on the gallows for those Chinamen, he'd felt reasonably self-satisfied. Now it all was changed. He found himself looking back on his start in the hangman trade. The way he'd been helped into it by the noted Texas "hanging judge," Orion Q. Partridge. Tree returned to home to east Texas after the war to find his father elected to sheriff. Signing on as his deputy, Zack helped his father keep the peace. But later in the year, when he'd been visiting in a nearby town, a drifter named Josh Pingree backshot Sheriff Aaron Tree.

Bent on revenge, Zack tracked down Pingree and brought him to justice. The owlhoot was tried and sentenced to hang. But the hangman was a blacksmith by trade and unskilled at execution. He used an old tree outside of town and strung Pingree up, strangling him unconscious but not killing him. The undertaker quickly put him in a pine coffin to bring him back to the town. An hour later, the jasper had escaped.

"Son of a bitch," Zack Tree now breathed. The hangman stepped to the window of his Deadwood hotel to survey the sky, darkening with the leaden clouds.

Same as that morning, down in Waco, Texas, he thought. After months of tracking, he'd finally given up on the pursuit of his father's killer — there were no more trails to trace. The bad *hombre* had simply vanished. Drifting down south, the young deputy wound up in Waco's Longhorn Saloon, nursing a full bottle of strong mescal. The kind with pickled worms that made a drinking man forget his troubles.

But he remembered it like it was yesterday when the portly figure of Orion Q. Partridge sat down next to him at the bar. The "hanging judge of Waco", he was a man of near sixty, sporting a rumpled Prince Albert coat and snowy white goatee. After calling for a drink, he'd introduced himself with some condolences about his old friend, Aaron Tree, and commenced to talking about the justice trade. By the next drink, he'd had Tree agreeing to work for him, learning the trade of lawful hanging.

Two years later, the elderly judge retired. Zachariah Tree took his new hangman's skills on the road. He would hang men properly under the law, without pain and until they were dead. Since the West was so burdened with human scum, he could be proud of his part in cleaning it. He vowed that what had happened to his father's killer would never happen at the end of Zachariah Tree's rope.

Now the hangman turned from the window and swiftly dressed himself. He had new ideas to follow up on. He'd consider them in the barber's chair while having a shave.

The man so proficient in giving haircuts was himself as hairless as a Mexican dog. At least on the top of his head, he was. The hands that were shaving the face of Zack Tree bore ash-hued fuzzy pelts. "Ahem," the barber coughed, not bothering to turn aside. "You were inquiring about local whorehouse owners?"

"I was," the hangman replied.

"Regarding Mr. Griswold," Barber Bob intoned. For a squat, toadlike shape, he had a rich, deep voice. " 'Cherry Creek Sam' Griswold, late of Denver, there the man goes. Headin' for the livery stable."

"Jesus!" Tree leaned forward in the chair and the thing gave a squawk and a jerk. "You mean that feller on the boardwalk?"

"Yeah, I do."

Tree tore the towel from his throat, and thrust it at the barber as he rose. The man with the razor stood back openmouthed.

Meanwhile Tree fixed the picture of the gent in question in his mind. Griswold was sixtyish, with a blocky shape. Stout, not flabby, heavily featured, and pink-skinned, as if kept from the sun. He rolled as he walked, like a grounded sailor. Today he wore a brown checked suit. Flat crowned hat. Riding gloves.

"Looks like a dude."

"But he ain't," asserted Barber Bob. "Come from ranching stock, he lived in Denver since right after the war, elected to the city council, got hisself bounced out. Knocked around with politics since, though I ain't heard quite exactly what. You heard, Alexander?"

The waiting customer was eager to pipe. "Nope. But Griswold was outta money when he drifted to these here parts. Started him all over agin. Dealin' monte in a tent."

"You've been help a-plenty, Bob," Tree said, paying the man with two liberty dimes. "Like the notion of a ride myself."

And he plunged through the door and out into the wind.

By the time he had dogged Griswold to the livery, the old pimp was already inside. On a hunch, the hangman decided to wait and watch. And sure enough, in a few minutes Griswold rolled out on a shiny buggy's seat. A solid bay trotter pranced between the shafts. The driver turned its nose north toward the main diggings.

The very route Tree had ridden yesterday.

Now Tree strode through the barn doors. He asked if he could have the same fine gray as yesterday.

"'Fraid not, Mr. Tree," Dan answered, looking sorry. Tree puzzled a minute, but then recalled. "The gray is rented, Mr. Tree. But there's a chestnut as is rested."

"Saddle it up. And I'm in a hurry."

Tree was trusting that Griswold could be overtaken, so he relaxed and rolled a quirly.

As the kid was tightening the cinch, Tree asked a question. "Feller just in, took him out a bay and rig?"

Dan fooled with the bit. "Mr. Griswold. Yeah."

"He go driving often?"

"No, not much," the kid replied. "But when he does, and it's me, not the owner, as tends him, he'll give me extra money. 'Don't spend it on loose females,' he always jokes." Dan shrugged and grinned. "Don't know what more I can tell you."

"You done enough, kid. I'd best get a move on. Well, *adios.*"

Tree swung to the saddle and gigged the chestnut up the street. Soon he was at the edge of town. This time he took more notice as he rode, and what he saw brought a disturbed, deep frown to crease his rugged features. Crossing Dolly Creek on a bridge of timbers, he scanned to his left, across a soggy, shallow swale. Between steep shale slopes lay an area that was jammed with shacks. The tiny, cramped structures were shoehorned in, wall abutting wall. Incredible. The dwellers were like tinned sardines.

When the combined odors of smoke and cooking fish reached Tree, he was able to put two and two together. The horse was carrying him past the Chinese district. Closer at hand now, he spotted shop signs in Chinese.

As he continued along the curving uphill route, he left Deadwood entirely behind at last, and again rode into the rougher country shaded by pines. It amazed him that the man he was following, Cherry Creek Sam Griswold, was able to make good time with the narrowness of trail, ruts, and low branches that had to play hob with any wheeled conveyance.

Tree wasn't overtaking, either, and part of the problem was the horse that Dan had provided him. The Chestnut, a thick-in-the-haunches, roman-nosed brute, didn't take to climbing easily, and balked at every step. Still, as the gulch continued in its northern curving sweep, Tree was convinced of the whorehouse owner's destination.

And then he rounded yet another bend and spotted the rig parked, canted in a ditch. The bay in the traces wasted to a convenient shrub.

They were at the foot of the hill that held the disputed gold claim. Griswold was not in view and had most likely hiked on up.

Palavering with the pair on guard, Tree told himself. He remained well short of the lookouts' field of view. He swung from the saddle and picketed the ornery mount. Leaning on the wheel of the buggy, Tree fell naturally into a comfortable, relaxed slouch. Voices could be heard up top, but the distance blurred the words.

Whatever Griswold's errand, it didn't take long. Zachariah Tree heard the crunch of boot soles, then saw the heavy man clumsily descending the treacherous path a few minutes later. Keeping his attention on the ground in front of him, though, the gent didn't immediately see the waiting man.

Then he drew up with a start. "What the hell — ?"

The hangman spoke crisply. "Cherry Creek Sam Griswold, ain't it? My name's Tree, and yeah, I followed you clear out here. And now I'm sure of a thing I only suspected. It's that you posted the gunsels on the claim. Chen and Fong's claim, ain't that c'rect?"

"Humph! Stand out of my way!" Tree was holding the bay horse's bridle, but the broad man moved quickly. He was on the sprung seat in an instant, flourishing the whip. The bay leaped in its harness. The hangman was flung clear.

In another second, the rig had vanished around the bend.

# Chapter Eight

"Hell," Zack Tree spat after the departing buggy. He was in the rented saddle of his rented mount without delay, but the animal started crow-hopping, fighting the bit, costing both time and patience to the rider. Tree finally got it under control and spurred into pursuit well behind Griswold in the direction of Deadwood.

A thrusting loaf-shaped hill caused the main trail to swing wide in its great curve. But now it was clear that a second trail existed, a game trail which cut off to the left and climbed on a smoother incline. Here could be the means for cutting off the fleeing buggy, he realized, coming back down to the Deadwood trail ahead of Sam Griswold and cutting him off.

Corralling Griswold to question him remained foremost still in Zack Tree's mind. With scarcely any hesitation, he reined the bronc up the game trail and gave the animal even more spur. The chestnut responded, and they plunged under pine boughs, and traversed dry gulches on their mad dash to cut off their quarry.

Both horse and rider were drenched with sweat as they pushed forward on the trail. A spooked mule-deer doe fled the path, and a short while later a large covey of quail did the same. They crashed a motte of pinyons and were forced to jump a deadfall at full speed.

Tree pulled his mount to stop as they crested a ridge to see a deep ravine below. "All right, you stubborn cayuse. We cross this one, then there's level riding on the other side."

The horse didn't descend the gulch slope willingly, but rather snorted, went wildly wall-eyed, and twisted its neck. "What the hell — ?" Then the chestnut lost its footing and tumbled, hurling Tree into the jumble of granite and clumped mesquite. The hangman rolled with the clawing branches raking him. His shirt was ripped, his Stetson lost. Pain lanced through his jarred, scraped body.

The hangman came to rest beside the horse, breath torn from his lungs by the force of the impact. He lay winded and motionless, then raised his head to catch a look about him.

The hammerheaded gelding was on its side, three legs thrashing, the fourth — the off-rear — twisted grotesquely. The limb was broken. Venting a low curse, Zack Tree put his knees under him, wincing, then climbed to a hobbling stand. The chestnut needed to be put out of its misery. He reached for his holstered Colt.

The thin-lipped mouth tightened imperceptibly as the man pointed the gun between the animal's pain-blurred eyes. He squeezed the trigger, and the .44 bucked, drilling the slug through the tough-boned skull. Blood gouted in a crimson splash from the hole, and the gelding shuddered and died. The sharp stink of expelled excrement flooded the air.

Zack Tree thought a minute on the problem of the saddle under the dead horse, then gave it up. Toting the thing back to town would give him a sore back as well as sore feet, he expected, and the sore hide he already had. Dan, the livery-stable kid, could ride to retrieve the stable's rented leather.

Tree paused to punch the spent shell from his Colt's cylinder and thumb in a replacement. Then he was ready to begin what was bound to be a tiring, long hike. He found the black hat a few feet away.

And then the sound reached his ears. A roar so faint at first that it was drowned by birdsongs in the brush. But it gathered strength second by second, until it turned into a powerful thunder.

Tree spun on the smooth floor of stones, looked behind him, but at first saw nothing. Nevertheless, he started to run. The side of the gulch seemed a mile away. His strong legs pumped, but seemed to make no progress. For sure it wasn't nearly enough. The hangman had observed flash floods before, but always from vantage points of safety. Now there was no safety, only the cold throb of certain death.

With the roar louder than ten express trains, the wall of water boiled around the bend upstream. Eight feet of rampaging water tossed whole oaks in the tide like toothpicks. Boulders were like play marbles in the surging tide. Tree forced his straining lungs to strain still more, his legs to pump still faster. Still the gulch wall remained beyond reach. Time was running faster than the man.

The hangman felt himself struck as if by a giant fist. He flew for a split second in a misting cloud of spray, then splashed in water. The water was high-country cold. Up in the higher country the night before, the rain had poured and poured for drowning hours.

And now Tree seemed doomed to drowning, as well.

Tossed and buffeted by the booming flood, the hangman did his best to swim, but was largely ineffective against the mighty force of current. Various kinds of debris swirled to all sides: tree branches, even the remains of dead elk, deer, rabbits. What appeared to have once been a miner's cabin swept past — and the water was still rising. The whipping, white-capped surface surged higher and higher. It wasn't going to stop. Tree tried to snare a floating log, but it rolled from him. A thrusting knob of shattered wood slammed his head.

His mind winked out.

Visions of his youth and young manhood passed before him in dazzlingly real flashes. He was a child at his mother's knee, and then a grown man standing sadly beside her casket. In another scene he was courting his schoolgirl sweetheart, and in the next staring down from horseback at his father's crumpled corpse. His father had been shot in the back. The corpse lay blood drenched by the wall of the cow town jail.

Suddenly, Tree's eyes popped open. Somehow, someplace, he was up and out of the rampaging flash flood. He saw that he lay soaked and exhausted on a sandy, sun-bathed bank. Beside him, the river's torrent flowed. He was alive.

"By God, I got thrown out of it!" He spoke to a sky that had changed from its lead color to a breathtaking cobalt blue. After a few more minutes reclining on the sand, he sat up, shook his head to clear it . . . and glimpsed something hovering over him from behind, a sight to jolt alarm signals through him.

A shadow was flung down across the sloping bank, and it was a shadow that moved. Tree threw his stiff, wet body into a swift, crawfishing move against a boulder, then he hauled upright with the last of his reserve strength, and launched himself. He rammed the standing man's form head on, and the two went down. Tree rolled on top and drew back with the tight-bunched fist.

"No! No hit me, mistah! Wait! Want help!"

Tree peered straight into the round, moonlike face of a young Chinese man.

"What the hell? Feller, you seen me down here, did you?" Tree scrambled to his feet and extended his hand to help the newcomer. Standing, Tree towered over the man come to render aid. To make up for the hard butt he'd thrown to the other's stomach, the hangman tried a friendly grin.

"More of my people up waiting on rim," the Chinaman said. He pointed, and Tree looked. He saw a whole group of bowing dark-skinned men with glossy pigtails and baggy clothes.

"Thanks for your concern, friend. Maybe you and your pards can get me back to Deadwood."

"Chinese people, we are taking you, mister. Got horse and li'l wagon. Too far for hurt man walking."

"I ain't all that banged up. . . ." Tree paused, feeling the bones ache in this shoulders and legs. "Well . . . all right, folks! I'd be glad to take your offer for a ride! Plumb beholden, in fact!"

It was the Chinaman's turn to smile, and he threw Tree a broad one. "Start now. Come, I show you path."

Tree let the friendly fellow lead the way up the rocky slope.

"Goodness me," Rebecca Dunmore said across the printer's table. Her fingers flew nimbly with the type she was setting. "Phil, are we really doing the true, right thing?"

"I do believe so." The newspaperman stood a few feet from his pretty wife, busily inking the old press they'd used to print the *Clarion*'s new run. There was a smudge of ink on his smooth, strong-lined cheek, and it gave his face a grim look.

"But doing this might be dangerous," the woman added.

"We've no choice, Becky."

She shrugged, jammed in place a line of ten-point to complete the boldface Gothic head. Then she worked at transferring what she'd just set from her type stick to the galley. The issue's front page was now bedded and ready. Phil Dunmore was wrestling with a bale of paper.

He paused, straightened, and peered over at Rebecca. "What that hangman said last night got me to thinking about our responsibility to the truth. If Chen and Fong didn't kill Jones and were hanged to cover some underhanded scheme, it's a newspaper's place to bring the matter to public attention."

"Very well. You know best, Phil." She paused and looked about the office. "I do wonder where Jory is."

"The lad's been absent on press days before. He could turn up late, still, with a lame excuse."

"Like the time he claimed the dog ate his trousers?" The woman's laugh tinkled.

"Or the occasion of his pa's birthday. When his father abandoned the mother before the boy was born." Phil Dunmore tightened the type bed with a key, loaded it onto the press, and levered through the first clean sheet. He held up the printed page, scanned it, and nodded his approval.

"Here we go, then, Becky, girl. This really reads well. Naming Griswold as the mysterious claim holder . . . why, if he's done wrong, it'll flush him into the open!"

# Chapter Nine

The helpful group of Chinese had taken Zack to his boardinghouse on returning to town and, after giving them a gold double-eagle in gratitude for their help, he'd gone straight up to change his clothes.

Tree figured he owed the livery for the killed chestnut, and planned to stop by and make payment soon. But the first item on his plate at the moment remained a gent by the name of Griswold. The desk clerk in his boardinghouse, after a handsome tip of one silver dollar, directed him to Miss Lil's, a prominent whorehouse reputed to be owned by the ex-Denver politician.

Tree passed along saloon row with a swing in his step. The street was crowded with the after-sundown throng of miners and townsmen drinking wildly and freely. Drunk men staggered across the boardwalk yelling and shooting off pistols. From the barrooms tinny music flowed, punctuated by an occasional crash or loud argument.

Ahead red lamps gleamed above the doorways of the parlor houses. A good many parlor houses. Tree headed straight for the rough log-and-canvas building with a big red L painted on the door. According to the clerk's description, this was Miss Lil's.

The plank door swung open on hinges of leather. Tree was greeted with a "Say, there! C'mon in!" The redhead with the husky voice wore a low-cut scarlet gown.

"Lookin' for a good time, big man? My name's Olive."

"I'm looking for your boss."

"Well, there sure ain't no real Miss Lil."

Tree snorted. "So I'm told. Then I'll settle for a gent named Griswold."

"Don't know as I recall gent by that moniker, honey," she said, smiling and looking over her shoulder to the back of the room.

Following her gaze, Tree saw them past the frilled, flouncy leg o' lamb shoulder of her dress: a duo of hardcases in serge frock coats and brocade vests. A lot of beef, by their look, and mean to boot. Judging from the bulges in their coats, both men were well armed. They looked about ready now to leave the corner at the slightest signal from the redhead.

Tree fished a silver cartwheel from his pocket and tossed it to the woman. She moved quickly with her hand, and caught the coin in midair.

"Well, you just found the key to my heart, cowboy. Any more where this came from?"

"Afraid not."

A sigh lifted heavy breasts beneath the silk. "If that's the case, then, you just got to follow me. It may look like we're heading to a crib, but I'll tell you when to turn."

He had been talking to the woman in the establishment's garish parlor. A number of worn-out sofas and hassocks stood about on a carpet that had seen better years. Only a few ugly women were in the room, mostly gone to flab and sag. Olive led the man in black past them without a glance, into a corridor of sorts. A series of sighs and lusty groans filtered from the cribs. The partitions were cheap, thin paste-board.

"That door's to the office," Olive said.

"Looks a mite stouter than some others."

"'Tis," the whore acknowledged. "Well, lots of luck to you, mister. With Cherry Creek Sam, you'll be needing it."

Tree rapped on the panel as soon as Olive had sashayed back the way she had come.

"Go way, Olive!" The voice within was familiarly gruff. "Now's the time to be taking care of customers. Though I got to admit I'm flattered!"

The hangman said nothing, only knocked again.

"I said I'm busy, you big-assed angel — "

When the door swung open and the bald man saw his visitor, his pink face flushed red. "You! The one as was up the gulch? Well, I wouldn't jaw with you this afternoon, feller, and I won't now!" He tried to shut the hangman out.

But Tree brushed past the man, and once inside the office, he stood stock-still. "See here, Griswold. You can call me Tree if you've got the mind." He let his hand poise near his six-gun butt, and eyed the stout man across a table. On the table lay a deck of cards, and beside it was a lamp. There was a door in the back that might lead to an alley.

Tree took note of the third man in the room, over on a bunk against a wall, lounging and grinning. Tree was careful not to turn his back on the hardcase bodyguard. Or either of the doors.

"I don't give a good shit what your name is," Griswold sniffed. "I just want you out of here, now."

Tree ignored the man. "I reckon you know I'm here to ask some questions of the one feller as can answer them. Same as I aimed to at the claim."

"I ain't got to answer — "

"First question," the hangman interrupted, "you came to Deadwood Gulch from Denver to join the gold rush. Word has it you got some claims under your name. Would the one the Chinamen Chen and Fong died for be one of them?"

A smile of recognition crossed Griswold's face. "Carl" — the stout man turned to the one lounging on the bunk, — "we got us the famous hangman name of Zachariah Tree right here in our office."

The lounger crossed one leg over the other, bringing the thigh up that wore the holstered six-gun. "I see the jasper, boss." Swinging to again face Tree, he said, "Shit, hangman, you're a feller after this old heart. A cool head, and you plumb got to have icewater in your veins. Why, from where I was in the crowd t'other day, it appeared your hand didn't shake a bit jerkin' that drop bar on them slant-eyed killers. Hell, I seen lynchings when — "

"Dammit, Griswold, I asked you a question."

The man from Denver was studying Tree closely, scratching his shiny bald pate. Tiny porcine eyes squinted, the inky pupils glittering. "Didn't figure you for a Chink lover, Tree. Else you just got you a big nose. Stick it in, that ain't no good. No good for me, no good for you. Ain't that right, Carl?"

"Right, boss."

Tree didn't bother to glance over toward the corner. "A feller as don't answer questions easy, he's most often got things to hide."

"Ain't got nothing to say to you, Tree." Griswold glanced at his pocket watch. "Now, I'm a busy feller. And your time is up. Best gather your ropes and leave Deadwood pronto. Lots of gunsels, niggers, yellow-skins, and Indians about the land who been askin' to meet old King Hemp."

Tree squared off his hat and looked straight at Griswold. "I reckon I'd be watching out for my own neck, if I were you, mister."

Carl jumped off the bed at that remark, but Tree simply raised his hands and walked out.

The hangman made his way through the narrow corridors back up front. And he was grinning. He had accomplished almost everything that he'd expected to.

No operator as slick as Griswold was about to spill his secrets for the asking. Tree had let him know he was onto him. Sooner or later the whoremaster would make his move, and he'd be there waiting.

When the hangman reached the bar, he paused a moment. He felt like a drink just for the hell of it before heading back for his hotel and a rented bed. The silver piece he had passed Olive ought to buy at least a swallow.

Looking around for the redhead, he spied somebody less pleasant by far edging his way.

If a gent could be described all mean and lean, the hard words fit this one. His six-foot-five height nearly nudged the canvas ceiling, though he slouched. The skin of his face, stretched drum tight, was peppered with smallpox scars. Two hands as scrawny and elongated as meat hooks swung and brushed the butts of matched Smith and Wessons Scholfield .45s.

As he approached Tree, the hangman adjusted his stance, half turned to face the string bean, his knees slightly bent. At an eyelid-flick's warning he could throw himself aside, at the same time drawing his own weapon and getting off a shot.

"Hold it right about there, Brace Haldane," the hangman rasped.

"Well, if it ain't Zachariah Tree, big as life." The tall man's voice was low and rumbling. As he stopped in his tracks, he eyed the hangman sharply.

"Long time, Haldane. Damned long time. Seen you last down El Paso way, I recollect."

"The Socorro Kid shoot-out."

"Some damned fine men ended up in boot hill."

Brace Haldane glanced right, and glanced left. The others in the room had found reason to move back toward the walls. The girls — now there were more of them — watched every move. The heavyset bouncers fingered empty glasses and fidgeted.

Zack Tree stood his ground, his right hand clawed and tense.

"So what now?" said Brace Haldane. "Far as I know, you ain't a badge packer no more, Tree. And way I see it, hangmen got no cause to judge other men or dig up the past."

"What's done is done, Haldane," Tree said. "I reckon Deadwood ought to be a big enough place for both of us."

"I'll always say the same thing: I reckon I always been faster than you. But if you see no need to try me, I can buy that." Haldane's smile was little more than a grimace. And then the tall man tugged the brim of his flat slouch hat.

Zachariah Tree watched him stroll across the room and retrieve a whiskey glass and a folded newspaper from a table by a window. He turned his back full on the hangman as he drank the firewater off. The gunfighter tucked the paper high between his side and upper arm, then headed directly for Griswold's office door.

The hangman wondered idly how the slouched man would take it when he wasn't allowed in. But Haldane pressed the latch, opened quietly, and glided inside.

Interesting, Tree thought, finishing his drink, and headed toward the door.

# Chapter Ten

The woman's voice, soft and furry in the deep bedroom gloom, wailed a moment at her height of passion and then subsided. Now silence reigned. Starlight penetrated the single window faintly, and the dark shapes of wardrobe, chiffonier, and rocking chair mere vague outlines. Out in the night, crickets chirred in the grass and shrubs, and the sounds were pleasant ones.

Phil Dunmore flopped back beside Rebecca on the mattress and sighed contentedly. Here was the coziest place he had ever known. It was where he took the joy offered by a loving wife, and gave joy in return. Although they were humbly furnished, these small, cramped rooms behind the *Clarion* office were a kind of heaven on earth to him.

The couple had been married for less than a year, and the days were still honeymoon days. The labor of putting out the paper could be exhausting, true, but there followed the long evenings, always spent together. Sometimes, as had happened tonight, the man would wake the woman in the hours before dawn, and the loving would be renewed.

Now the woman stirred on the far side of the feather tick. "Phil, I believe I heard a noise."

"Sure you did. I was purring like a big old cat."

"No! I'm serious. Outside, around in front, I guess there might have been a — "

This time it was an unmistakable crashing that rent the night quiet. A heavy object had shattered the cracked front windowpane of the *Clarion* offices.

Phil Dunmore jerked upright and hurtled out of bed, his nightshirt flapping. Crossing the floor in the dark, he stubbed his bare foot, smothered a curse, and slammed into the doorside bureau with yet another painful thump. But his hand was at the drawer now, opening it with a yank to clutch the smooth metal shape within.

He had always kept his father's old dragoon pistol cleaned, oiled — and loaded. On the frontier it was a matter of simple protection. But he'd never fired it. Now he drew the weapon's hammer to cock, stepped to the bedroom door, and hissed over his shoulder to his huddling wife.

"Stay here, Becky. I'll go investigate, call you if you're needed, or if it's safe. Otherwise, I'll expect you to hide out here. I'll be back shortly."

"Oh, Phil, be careful! I don't know . . ."

But he was gone, and she let her voice trail off. She ran her fingers through her tangled hair and tugged her night shift. Then she sat back and wrung her small, strong hands.

Meanwhile her husband advanced into the front printshop area as dark as pitch.

Across the room, a sulfur match flared. When the small flame touched to a pine-knot torch, the room turned bright. The torch was held by a man whose head was shrouded in a sack. Behind cut holes, his eyes shone wickedly. Masked men stood to either side of the first one. A fourth intruder was crawling across the glass-strewn sill.

"Say, you men — " Phil Dunmore called.

"Well, looka here!" The head gunnysacker laughed. "Our runt-o'-th'-litter publisher, by God! You come to bust up what we're doin'? Mebbe *you'll* get busted up! Haw!"

"I've got a gun!" Dunmore waved the heavy firearm. "And I'll use it! I warn you — "

"Horseshit!"

Massing together in a human wedge, the men in the bunch charged. Dunmore, trying to trigger, was overwhelmed and the gun was grabbed from his grip. He found his slender frame shoved against a table laden with typecases. A fist shot out and drove into his nose.

Dunmore felt the quick flood of hot blood. His mouth filled with a coppery taste. Another fist slammed his breastbone, and the air rushed from his lungs in a painful gust.

A blow to Dunmore's jaw whipped his head back, and an explosion of pain wrapped his brain in a fiery crimson cloud. Someone hit him with a chair, which smashed in a shower of splinters. Another masked *hombre* followed with a punishing gut punch. The publisher was flung left and right, shoved from one intruder to another, each dealing hurt in his own way, each blow worse than the last. The room was filled with rough laughter and the *thud-thud* of bunched knuckles on flesh. Two gunnysackers pinned Phil Dunmore's arms. The newspaperman was helpless against the rain of brutal blows. As he retched and grunted, a knobby knee pumped up. Dunmore's groin took the impact, and the newspaperman screamed.

"Hey, hush your mouth, feller!"

"Callin' passersby? Mebbe you just need you a gag!"

Stooping to the floor where it was littered with spilled printing type from the upset compositor's table, the leader of the gang of intruders filled a hand with the small squared-off pieces of molded metal. Then the man shoved a palmful of sharp metal into Dunmore's mouth.

The newspaperman choked for a few seconds, then suddenly went limp and slid to the floor.

*'Phillip!'* Becky Dunmore screamed, grabbing the attention of murderous gang.

"Say, there she is! Grab the gal, boys. Now the *real* fun can start."

The woman was paralyzed with fright. Pairs of hamlike hands clutched, squeezed, and pulled her as she was battered like a mere rag doll. Bruising blows fell on her arms, breasts, and thighs. All the hardcases wanted her all at once and stretched out on the floor next to her dead husband.

Callused fingers clawed the sheer neckline of her garment, prepared to pull . . .

"Hey, in there!" a man's voice sounded from outside, then a small crowd of angry voices joined in. "What's the ruckus? Someone breaking in?"

"I'm a deputy, folks!" a louder gruff voice rasped. "Let me through, and I'll get to the bottom of this!"

"That window right there's busted all to hell! Newspaper office, Deputy!"

"Could be a robbery!"

There were faces at the window, and there was pounding on the door, but the door that was firmly barred. Still, it wouldn't take more than a few minutes before the Deadwood neighbors broke the panel and poured on in.

Through the eyeholes in their hoods, the would-be rapists exchanged glances. Then their leader burst out. "We got to hightail!"

In a flash the woman was abandoned where she lay, hardcases scrambling to their feet. "Through to the back, boys! Out the window in the bedroom! Rattle your hocks!"

As the front wood split open and the crowd rushed through, the last of the murderers escaped through the back window. In the lead was a plump man with a nickel badge, the night-rounds deputy. Shopkeepers, clerks, and tradesmen stumbled in on the lawman's heels.

"My God!" "The newspaper plant been busted to hell!"

"Look, over in the corner is the publisher's wife! Why that poor li'l thing!"

The blond, half-naked woman could only crouch on the floor and sob. A blacksmith's shirt was thrown quickly over her bruised, bare shoulders.

"What's been happening?" barked the deputy.

"Let her alone, Sylvester!"

"Damn it, somebody did this! Where'd they go?"

"Out the rear!"

"Guns out, fellers. We'll get back there on the double!"

The lawman and a few others exited with a loud racket of stomping boots. The men who remained gathered tightly around the hurt woman. "Did we get here in time?"

"In time for what?"

"T' save her honor!"

"Looks to be!"

Rebecca Dunmore sobbed. "Phil! My Phil!"

"Where's the husband?"

"Over in the corner!"

The men stood grouped beside the toppled printing press, their eyes cast downward. An uncomfortable quiet had seized the group. A stifled cough turned into a stifled retching.

"Will he be all right? Will my Phil be all right?" The woman pushed her way and elbowed as they tried to keep her back. On her lips rose a hysterical wail. "Oh, please *let me* — "

But well-meaning townsfolk kept her back. "Ma'am, he's done crossed over."

"Must've happened when the press toppled," another said.

"Plumb heavy machine. Dunmore's chest, it's all busted — "

Becky collapsed.

"She's fainted!"

"Fetch the doc,' someone called out.

Bob the barber scampered to the door himself, and ran on out into now-brightening, new dawn.


Zachariah Tree sat at the check-clothed cafe table and unfolded the newspaper. His morning cup of coffee rested by his arm untouched, its misty fragrance drifting unnoticed toward the ceiling. Eyes of prison-bar gray surveyed the columns of the print, racing over the front page, pausing at the bolder headings. His gaze found the boxed center spread, and he read more closely. This was it. Pure dynamite.

A waitress behind a grimy but frilled apron showed her fishlike face. "What's your pleasure for breakfast, sir? Steak and eggs? Well *sure*, we got fresh eggs, dime apiece."

"Come back in a minute or so, won't you, gal?" He scarcely looked up at her. After a few second's wait, she stalked off in a huff.

"Gold Claim Skullduggery?" the headline read. Samuel Griswold, Local Kingpin, Tied to Mystery Murder Claim.

Tree read swiftly through the rest of the news article, and then the hangman slapped the copy of the *Clarion* down. Having written such, he decided, the Dunmores could be in danger. More danger than they knew.

He cursed himself for not buying and reading the sheet last night. His mind had been on his visit to Griswold then, but that was no excuse. He should have sensed the mischief in the situation when he'd spilled the beans to the Dunmore couple, the news that Cherry Creek Sam owned the salted claim. As it was, the couple had lost no time with the story, had gone and printed it. Damned do-gooders, Tree swore silently, and rushed out of the cafe to the newspaper offices.

As he hurried along the Main Street boardwalk, he was caught in an excited group of people blocking his way. They stood in front of a door that bore the lettered sign: Doctor's Office.

"Trouble?" he asked one person.

"Dammed right," an old-timer in a patched coat said. "Had us two beatings here in town overnight. A couple, a man and a woman, got pounded bad. And the wrongdoers busted up their place all up, besides."

Zack Tree's brow folded into a concerned frown. "What couple? And what place?" The hairs at his nape had started a warning prickle that he had felt often enough before.

"Why, the newspaper feller and his missus," injected a bystander. "I was there when the deputy come! Seemed he heard yells and such, clear over to the Alamo Saloon!"

"Good God!"

"Ain't nothin' good 'bout what happened to that pair. Looks to've been a crew as worked 'em over. The husband's dead and the poor gal near ruined, half naked, in that thin, torn camisole! And the owlhoot outfit seems to've got away!"

"I'm going in there," Tree snapped huskily, grabbing the doorknob, turning it and pushing the panel open on the doctor's crowded office. Standing over a cot was Mike Wilmer. Beside the lawman was a middle-aged gent with a kindly, creased face. The doc's eyes were serious behind his thick-lensed steel-wire wire spectacles.

"How's Mrs. Dunmore?" the hangman demanded.

For some reason, the marshal chose to answer. "The wife, she's shook up bad." Tree peered past the others.

"I've given sedative powders to the woman," the doctor said. "She's better off knocked out than hysterical, any day."

Tree nodded, then turned to Wilmer. "You gathering a posse, Marshal?"

"Won't do no good now, Tree. Them varmints got too long a lead."

"Got to be somethin' the law can do, ain't there?"

"I'll think on it, but don't seem like there's — hey!"

All he could see was Zack Tree's back pushing through the crowd.

# Chapter Eleven

Tree walked along the Main Street boardwalk of deadwood, turning the corner at the partly constructed new bank, then moving on along to pass a series of small shops. There was the barbershop, an apothecary's shop, and that ever-present fixture of a mining-boom camp; the assayer. The hangman passed them all without a sidelong glance, his mind wrapped in his racing thoughts.

Then he was moving down along saloon row, and his brain turned to patterns: patterns of events, patterns of involved people — even the pattern of the shabby lawman's work in the roaring gold-rush town. The possible miscarriage of justice in the hanging of the Chinamen had meant nothing to Marshal Mike Wilmer. And

98

now the man seemed all primed *not* to find Phil Dunmore's slayer. Wilmer was a stupid and disagreeable jasper, true, but it wasn't all that clear to Tree whether he was really crooked.

Putting the blame for the bust-up of the *Clarion* on violent folks who happened to hate Chinese was an easy explanation, and not unreasonable, either. Tree acknowledged that he'd had to deal with that wild Irishman and crew the time he'd first met Phil. And yet, the Chinese-hater notion left out Griswold, the man the newspaper accused last night.

It remained for him to ask Rebecca for a description of the attackers. If one were tall and lean and had a pockmarked face, that man could be Brace Haldane. But the identification would need to wait until she was awake, and that left some time on the hangman's hands.

In front of a saloon called the Queen of Sheba he turned in, pushing through a set of brightly painted bat-wings to confront a long and almost-empty barroom. Last night's strewn sawdust hadn't yet been swept, and the air reeked of stale whiskey and puke.

As good a place as any, Zack, Tree thought, to start a trace-down of the past of a man called Jones. A slick-haired bartender from the old mold spoke across the shiny mahogany. "What's your pleasure, mister?"

"A schooner of cold beer would go good — and some palaver." Tree had a silver dollar that he liked to take out and finger on such occasions. At the moment, it was seeing hard action.

The bar dog stared suspiciously. "Ain't house policy for me to stand and flap my jaws. I just lay down the drinks."

Tree flipped the coin and caught it again. "I'm just asking about a feller name of Alonzo Jones."

"Never heard of him."

"Forget the beer."

Not much of a waster of time, the hangman stalked straight outside.

The next saloon in the row was the Red Dog. Here the same query got the same answer — and with hardly less surliness.

Success five stops later.

"Jones? Yeah. Sure," grumbled the bar dog at the dive called the Elephant. The fellow with the drooping moustache leaned confidentially forward as he polished a glass with a greasy towel.

"Yeah, sure — what?"

"You handin' across that there dollar?"

"Here. But this better be good."

"The best. Jasper you're after, he's plumb dead."

"I'm a patient man, and I'm a-waiting."

"That's all I got to say."

Tree's hand shot out rattler-quick, and he had the bar dog by his high, stiff collar. He wasn't gentle as he jerked "Moustache's" face close enough to breathe in. "*I* don't happen to think it's all you got to say. No more than I got nothing to do today than grind you up and spit you out, feller. Want to try again?"

Brawny as "Moustache" looked under the starched shirt, he caved in. "I-I, er, say, let me go!"

"Alonzo Jones?" Tree lightened his grasp's force, but kept the bar dog in tow.

"W-well — Jones'd come in here some. Play cards from time to time — penny-ante stuff. Five-card draw. Drank cheap trade whiskey that we sell, and never complained."

"What else?"

"Er, well, there was Nell."

A tightening of Tree's powerful grip. "And this Nell, she is — ?"

The man slumped, all resistance gone. "A fat horse-face as works upstairs. The owner lets her use one of the cribs for the usual cut. Nell was some sweet on ol' Alonzo, and dished him out good times for free. If you could call 'em good times."

"And she upstairs in the Elephant now?"

"No, she ain't here now, she went out. Prob'ly be back tonight. Yeah, come back tonight, mister, along about nine. Nell, she can tell you all about Jones. And she can't force you to get in bed — not a big, tough *hombre* like you are."

Tree released the man, who looked relieved. "And you won't tip her off to expect me?"

"Aw, why the hell'd I do a thing like that?"

As he left, Tree smiled inwardly. By his Waterbury fob watch it was time to go, check on the Dunmore woman.

Rebecca was sitting up in the doc's softest chair,

and had brushed out the rich blond hair. Unbound, it haloed her fine head and fell over the squared shoulders in a shimmering cascade. She was wearing a comfortable dress which the doctor must have sent for, probably from her own home.

She would have looked normal but for cheeks wet with streaming, shining tears.

"I reckon the medical man told you about Phil," Tree said upon entering the room. "I didn't know your husband long, ma'am, but he sure seemed a right fine man." It was the kind of thing that you told a newly widowed woman, he supposed. There was no sense sending her off into hard, distraught bawling. Not if he wanted clear information.

"My Phil was a wonderful man, and a wonderful husband, Mr. Tree. I plan to continue putting out the *Clarion*, don't hesitate to say. Phil loved that paper near as much as he loved me, and my efforts shall be my best tribute."

"All right with me, ma'am. Now, I got to tell you, my first interest is to find Phil's killers — the same men as done the beating of you and the wrecking of your office. Can you give me any help?"

Sitting stiffly, she shuddered. "There were four men, and their heads were hidden by sacks. No one could have recognized them. All had rough voices, and used foul language."

"Unusual clothes?"

"Rough clothes. Boots. Pistols at their belts."

"Anybody very short or very tall?"

102

"Not noticeably. No."

So Haldane hadn't been along, apparently, Tree took thoughtful note. "What else?"

"I'm afraid that's all. They seemed to want to wreck the premises, and hurt Phil and me. . . ."

"Never mind saying any more that's painful now," he told her. "I'll be talking to you again, letting you know anything I dig up."

"That awful Marshal Wilmer hasn't been back. It's almost as if he thinks we brought all this trouble on ourselves, Phil and I. I know that the newspaper sometimes printed things Deadwood didn't agree with, but as a lawman, don't you think — ?"

"Yeah, I do happen to think the law ought to be plumb fair. There's a thing called justice, only sometimes it seems hard to find. Well, Mrs. Dunmore — "

"Call me Becky. And you'll come tomorrow to Phil's burying, won't you?"

"Oh, I'll be there, Becky."

He saw no harm in humoring her.


The upstairs hallway above the Elephant was far from well lit, and Tree walked it carefully. Nevertheless, his boots seemed to ring like drumbeats in the stale confines over the saloon. The barroom noises from below were subdued at the early hour, and filtered up faintly.

He counted the doors as he moved forward, since he had been told that the one to Nell's crib was the fourth from the stairs. When he reached it, he knocked.

103

"Yeah, come on in, darlin' !"

The blowsy woman lay on the old, chipped bedstead, clad in a saffron-colored wrap that looked ready to fall open at the throat. Tree sincerely hoped that wouldn't happen. He'd had enough of gruesome sights recently. "You the gal called Nell?"

"That's me, all right, mister. Say, you ain't such a bad appearin' one."

"I've been told it before, for one reason or another."

"Well, you talk some waspish, for a gent carryin' notions of a good time. You got a good time on your mind, mister? Or if you ain't, just state your business."

"You knew a jasper named Alonzo Jones, now dead."

"I did."

"If you're willing to talk about him, I'd be willing to make it worth your while."

A sly grin crossed the mouth. "I like things as're made worth my while. Go on."

"Rumor says he got killed over a claim owned by Sam Griswold — "

Suddenly, the door slammed open, and in rushed a man. A burly giant of man, red haired, slab faced, and scowling. Zack Tree spun to confront the newcomer. "You're the feller as hates Chinese. I saw you at the *Clarion* office, making trouble for the Dunmores! What — ?"

Paddy Riley pulled a knife from the top of his muddy stovepipe boot, gave a grizzly's outraged cry and closed in on Tree in the confined quarters, slashing with the Bowie's blade.

Nell Conway shrieked like a ruptured banshee.

# Chapter Twelve

Although Zack Tree's hand streaked for his Colt, he was hampered for want of elbow room. He had to sidelong suddenly to avoid the newcomer's first knife thrust, and heaved up with a grunt and a crash against Nell Conway's bed. Then the oversized slattern chose to buy in, clutching leechlike to the hand that clawed for the six-gun.

"Goddamn!" The hangman shook her off, but the .44 went with her. All three of them in the tiny whore's crib heard it clank to the floor.

"Ah, now I got ye, villain!" Paddy Riley's big round face loomed pumpkinlike. "No gun, no knife o' yer own! Why, I'll slice your guts out, hang' em up like laundry!" And again he moved with all the swiftness of a crazy bull.

But this lunge, too, missed the man in black, who, as well as dodging, shoved the female as far as possible from danger's path. "Laundry, hey? Best watch your own!" Tree kicked high and hard with a bootheel, to connect solidly with Riley's thigh. The Irishman roared and retreated a mere half step.

"Stand back, Nell! I'll tend to you later, by God!"

Tree tried a feint with an arm.

Paddy Riley wasn't fooled. He waded in flat-footed, the big Bowie waving like a boatman's paddle. An upward slice with the blade opened the sleeve of Tree's shirt from the wrist to the elbow. He felt a sting, and a rush of hot blood down the forearm. It was only a nick. He reached rattler-quick, and grabbed his opponent's knife arm to draw the man in. But instead of releasing the knife, the Irishman yanked free, spun, came on again.

Another kick and shove fended him, giving Tree the time to deliver a slamming one-two combination of punches to the towering bastard's midsection.

Paddy Riley howled and flung backward, nearly off his feet. But he recovered himself before being propelled clear out the door and fetched up against the jamb instead. The Irishman came off the door, slashing left to right, fortunately missing as the hangman dodged away yet another time. Tree yanked the pillow from the woman's bed and spotted a knife and grabbed it.

The Irishman was feinting, moving in again, but this time Tree was armed and slashing. "Come on and get it," the hangman hissed. "Or are you scared, feller?"

Paddy Riley twisted suddenly and slashed at Zack Tree's face. Tree hooked his leg behind Riley's leg, and threw his weight to bring the big wild Irishman down. Tree forced his knife to Riley's chest and heaved. At the same moment the giant gave a mighty upward lurch. . . .

There was a gasp, as of silent pain, and Tree's arm was drenched with hot, red blood. The curved blade had plunged deep, almost to the hilt. The Irishman shuddered and lay dead on the floor.

Tree got to his haunches, abandoning the weapon where it stuck. He caught Nell as she tried to bolt.

The woman hunkered on the bed, peering at him. Then she peered down at Paddy Riley, her eyes dry, but blurred and fixed. "You killed my man, mister?"

Tree could only nod. "Looks that way. Some would say he killed himself." The hangman climbed all the way to his feet now, and thrust his face close to the haggard woman's. He already heard footfalls and excited voices out in the whorehouse corridor, and knew that he wouldn't have much longer to get his answers out of Nell.

In the guttering light, the handle of the death knife stood straight upright from the corpse. The lamp's rays caught and reflected on the haft's deep carvings. Tree came quickly to the point. "Where'd you get the Chinese knife?"

Nell cringed, but didn't respond.

"*I said —* "

"Oh, awright," the whore croaked in her throat. "I got the sticker from Alonzo. Gave it me before died, he did. Had him two or three of 'em in his poke."

"Jones just happened to own several Chinese knives?"

She nodded. "Curios, you know."

"Well, I reckon I know it now." Tree pressed on. "Woman, Jones and Sam Griswold, those two ever get together? Friends, maybe?"

"Friends? Alonzo couldn't stand Cherry Creek Sam! Owed him too much from the gambling on the cards!"

"Uh-uh," Tree said, closing it off.

The door to the crib burst open much as it had before, and yet another face peered in. "Well, I'll be damned! Is that you, Tree?" Face and voice belonged to Marshal Mike Wilmer, who rushed on excitedly. "Whore in the next crib said there was a ruckus and . . .

"Self defense."

"Of that I got no doubt."

Wilmer motioned to his deputies, and now they too crowded in the crib. "Paddy Riley, hey," the top law-dog crowed. "Well, Mr. Hangman, you got you Phil Dunmore's killer. Been looking for the town's top Chinaman hater, by god!"

Tree frowned. "Figure the case is all wrapped up, Wilmer?"

"Looks like. I'm thankin' you, Deadwood's thankin' you too."

Tree shook his head. "Why?"

"Hangman, you saved the town from the bother of a trial!"

# Chapter Thirteen

The sun was bright through clouds thin as
mare's tails, and the heat was stoking up. The
burial of Phil Dunmore's mortal remains was
slated for high noon.

The hangman was up earlier than that, however, but not by much, after sleeping through a
night cut short with planning. He shaved himself in the cold water of the washstand, since
barbers often tended to take their time. He
didn't want to be late on this occasion, for his
own sake as well as for Rebecca Dunmore's. He
was determined to get answers to some tough
questions from the jaspers still around town,
once the corpse was planted,

So he tugged on a fresh, starched shirt, white
as a December snowfall, knotted his string tie

under the turned-down collar, and finally donned his freshly brushed black frock coat. He dusted his black Stetson with the towel from the commode, and descended to bid the desk clerk a curt "Good day."

After a heavy breakfast at a cafe called the Comet, he headed toward the cemetery at the town's south margin arriving with less than five minutes to spare. He strode past the hearse that had been pulled to a stop on the narrow strip of scraggly green grass, scanning it again, this time struck by the well-used look of the grim conveyance. One of the beveled glass side windows was cracked. The black lacquer finish wore a front-to-rear pocking of deep chips and scratches.

The undertaker in Deadwood did a lot of business, as everyone was aware. The condition of his equipment proved it.

The high and scorching sun was making Tree sweat, but he doubted that the undue warmth was what had kept the folks away. A group of four had gathered about the grave behind the rusty fence of iron pickets. Tree moved to join the doctor, undertaker, preacher, and widow.

Rebecca Dunmore was a golden-haired vision. The bruises from her beating had faded, and the facial swelling was erased. She wore a mourning dress of black bombazine. The matching hat was of funereal crepe.

Behind the hearse, with its black, wind-flagged ostrich plumes, two gravediggers lurked.

"It appears we're ready to get started," the preacher said. He was the same one who had turned green at Chen and Fong's hanging. Bible thumpers were a rare breed in churchless mining towns, and this one seemed more comfortable with the task at hand. "The Lord giveth, and the Lord taketh away," the rich, deep voice intoned, honed by much practice. Instead of listening to the empty-sounding words, the hangman let his gaze wander. The doc appeared properly solemn. Undertaker Bosley's studied sober look was as expressive as a drawn-on mask.

He had to have been working late, Tree knew, on the brand-new corpse he had been given: Paddy Riley, Irishman, deceased. But he stood at the end of the closed pine coffin with a stiff spine, wide-eyed.

The hangman had never met a funeral maker who had much to say on the subject of death. The crew were a close mouthed lot. Not unlike professional executioners.

"So, may the dearly departed rest in peace. Amen. Ashes to ashes and dust to dust." The preacher was emptying a handful of the gritty stuff over the bouquet atop the coffin — wild lupine, pitiful, although plentiful. The hangman got set to take his leave.

"Thank you so much, Mr. Tree, for coming," said a voice which he recognized as Rebecca Dunmore's. Tree turned to meet her open face tilted upward toward his, and he could see the damp streaks that the tears had made. Even then, twin drops were poised at the corners of her emerald eyes.

"Nothing at all, ma'am. I had the pleasure of knowing your husband. It was fitting that I come to his burying."

"Not many folks in Deadwood feel as you do, I'm afraid. Many disliked the controversial stands that the paper took. Like the issue of the treatment of the Chinese." She glanced about woefully. "Still, to have a turnout so poor . . . I wouldn't have thought — "

"Best not to think too much just now, Rebecca," Tree suggested. "Get you a bit of good rest. Start packing things for your trip back East."

"*What? Back East?*" Suddenly Rebecca Dunmore bristled. "Why, I'm not going back East with my tail between my legs! Phil wouldn't want it! As I mentioned to you earlier, I intend to push on with publishing the sheet!"

"But — "

The woman continued emphatically. "The *Clarion* is a labor of love! Why, I intend to toil all this afternoon, sorting messed type, putting things back in order! I've even hired the blacksmith to repair the Excelsior press. The next issue will be out in only a week, maybe less."

"Then, I wish good luck to you, Rebecca."

A brisk nod. "For my success? I'm much obliged, I'm sure."

As he trudged across the barren, weedy plot, he waved at preacher and doctor both. Each seemed wrapped in his own thoughts.

Zack Tree turned into the office of another assayer he'd selected. A large lamp burned despite the bright daylight hour. It seemed an emblem of professional success, and Tree felt good about his choice.

Assayers, he knew, came in all shades of reputation, honesty. About the same as every occupation on God's green earth.

On a counter against the back wall were arrayed all the needed tools for the analysis of promising ore. Scientific apparatuses of one kind or another filled the broad, flat surface: delicate scales in a glass case, dark brown bottles large and small, a clutch of odd-shaped vials. On a stool perched a man in overalls, a small mustache adorning a youngish, intelligent face. All the fellow's concentration, for the moment, was directed at the things he was fiddling with. Tree spoke up. "I'm looking for the assayer."

The man glanced quickly over his shoulder, then back to his labors. Various rock samples were spread on metal trays, and deft hands were sorting, moving things about.

"Be with you in a bit. Right now I'm in the midst . . . " Words broke off, and concentration was resumed.

Minutes passed.

Zachariah Tree's nostrils sucked in strange chemical fumes.

He had to quell the urge to sneeze. Finally the assayer had his samples and gear arranged to his satisfaction. Again swiveling on the stool to face the hangman, he managed a shy, thin smile.

"I'm Garth Henderson, assayer by profession, and of course, you're in my laboratory, such as it is. How can I help you, mister? May I assume you're a miner, and you've brought around some specimens for testing?"

Tree chuckled inwardly at the educated manner of speech. Henderson talked a lot like the unfortunate Phil Dunmore. He had that same fresh, young look — of one intending to one day set the world on fire.

But outwardly the hangman kept his expression blank, even sour. "Not along with me, no. No samples, Henderson, leastways not at the moment. You see"— a conspiratorial pause — "let me be frank. I ain't a miner — yet. Just about to jump into the game, though. Since just now I don't happen to know a whole lot, I figure I need help. And that's where you come in."

"Well, it's my business," the assayer said, "to analyze ore samples and predict the eventual yield of the ground they're gathered from. I'm good at what I do, I'll confess, and strictly honest. An assayer's word, even on the certificates he writes, is only as good as his reputation."

"You sound about the kind of man I'm looking for," the hangman affirmed. "Now, if I knew a little on how you go about things — "

"I guess you *are* new on the diggings, Mr. . . . er . . . "

"The name is Tree."

"Mr. Tree, I'm running a test for a client now, as a matter of fact. You're welcome to observe."

"I'd be beholden."

"It goes like this." Garth Henderson shoved a glass beaker under Zack Tree's nose to show him the contents, a gritty powdering of crushed rock, mixed gray and umber. "Here are scrapings from the nugget I was brought. I'll be applying aqua regia, an acid that'll dissolve what precious metals might be present. Now." The assayer added a few drops from a small brown bottle. He waited, then added another substance, creating a sudden puff of smoke.

"No difficulty, Mr. Tree. The experiment is going quite normally. So let's see here what we have. Oh-ho! Virtually nothing!"

The hangman's eyes joined Garth Henderson's in studying the residue swirling about in the glass container. It contained nothing much different from what had been present at the start. "Mr. Tree, if the specimen had contained gold, we'd be seeing it now, flecks sinking to the bottom of the neutralized medium. When my client is informed his claim is not going to pay to work, well, there'll be one more disappointed man in Deadwood, town of a thousand broken dreams."

"So all it takes is a few minutes."

"Yes. You've seen all there is to see."

Tree stood back, straightened his jacket, straightened his hat, and fixed Garth Henderson with a sincere, straight look. "Mr. Assayer, I'll likely be stopping back. You're here most of the time?"

"Even my sleeping quarters are on the premises. Of course, I don't appreciate midnight wakeups, but on any other occasions, I'll be glad to help."

Out in the street the air was purer than in the stuffy lab, and Tree took a long, pleasant sniff, then paused to roll and light a quirly. He filled his lungs with the pungent bluish smoke from the Union Leader, then strode off on the next errand that he had set for himself.

Judging from the looks of the path that led up to it, the dwelling of Judge Enos Depew appeared much the same. Tree had last seen it on his angry visit just after the hanging of Chen and Fong. Now he dug stiff boot soles into the muddy ruts left by runoff on the grassless slope, put leg muscles behind the climb, and mounted steadfastly. At one point he heard the sharp crack of a twig behind him, but turned and saw nothing.

A rabbit or squirrel, he assured himself, and went on ahead, whistling between clenched teeth.

When he reached the crest, he walked clear around the small house and noted the small evidences of neglect: a pile of refuse, a privy door hanging by a single hinge. He could not see in through the drawn curtains, but the fact didn't affect him much. He pounded loudly on the door, and stood quietly on the front porch awhile. Getting no answer, he tried the door, found it unlocked and entered.

A deep, clammy silence filled the front room. The hangman moved to the window, drew back the crocheted curtain, and let bright sun through the fly specked panes. Then he proceeded to the bedroom, where he found his man.

Depew, in a sweat-stiff, soiled nightshirt, lay on the bed. His bare feet, bulging with bunions, poked over the footboard. The old, unshaven judge roared out a long, hoarse snore.

"Enos! Goddammit! Enos!" The hangman crossed to his prospective source of information, grabbed the old-timer's shoulders, and shook him roughly.

Another snore sounded, then the snort of a person arousing from drunken sleep. Tree's foot kicked an empty brandy bottle and sent it spinning crazily across the floor. The container clinked against another overturned one.

"Huh? What? Zack?"

"Well, at least your eyes are open. Christ, but they're bloodshot."

Enos Depew sat up, ran a hand across his face. The fingers seemed to hang up in the seams. "Yeah, you do look a mite reddish to me, young feller." The magistrate shook himself like a drenched spaniel. "If'n I could have some of the hair — "

"Of the dog that bit you? Would it help you think clear?"

"You bet!"

"In the cupboard, I suppose? Well, come on into the parlor. You're disgusting as hell, you know that? I only came back on account of you may have answers for me."

"Zack, boy, old times . . . "

He stopped still in the shoe box of a hallway and stared into the old-timer's watery eyes. "Far as I'm concerned, Enos Depew, old times between you and me don't happen to signify much no more. The dead folks are piling up everyplace I turn in this damned town, and it all started with the hanging I done of that pair of Chinamen. You *do* remember Chen and Fong?"

"Er, yeah . . ."

The pair were in the parlor now. Tree found himself supporting the weak-kneed old judge, who had stumbled on the hooked rag rug. Depew was trembling, but it couldn't have been from cold, the hangman decided. Rather the after effects of the stomach-rotting liquor Enos had lately made his life. He propped the sot against a chair.

"Stand here! Yeah, if you didn't remember Chen and Fong I'd figure you for loco. The trial you gave the pair ought to haunt you plenty, since the real killer or killers of Alonzo Jones are likely still strolling around, saucy as unbroke colts. I want you to tell me first about the bastard Griswold, second about what happened to the money Chen and Fong paid for the salted claim."

Without warning, the window exploded, driving glass across the room in a sheeting sliver shower. At the same instant, the face of the judge was slammed by a bullet. Inches from his own face, Tree saw Depew's livid in death, in the middle of his brow, a new, bloody eye.

Another shot boomed, and another slug drove in, this one blowing off Tree's hat, and then the attacker's fusillade began in earnest.

# Chapter Fourteen

Another slug of heavy, hot lead and then another tore through the house, blowing away the rest of the wide-silled side window, piercing the plank siding, and letting loose hails of splinters. Tree's hand behind Depew, slick with gore, let the old man's corpse drop. Since bullets were still buzzing like wasps about the judge's parlor, Tree dropped flat beside the dead man. He crabbed hurriedly to one side as he clawed for his six-gun.

He came around with the big Colt as he fetched up hard against the legs of the heating stove. Just above him a bullet slammed the cast iron, and zinged off in a ricochet.

Tree suddenly scrambled to the wall, raised his head, and peered through the glassless frame.

Another shot forced him to duck.

But he had glimpsed what he had wanted: the location of the hidden gunman. A blue smear of smoke hung above a particular mesquite clump in the shade of an alder a dozen or so yards away.

It seemed as though the attacker had given himself a perfect setup and had made a perfect shot.

Unless the lead slug had been meant for Tree! The notion struck the hangman as he crouched, his Colt's butt plates glued to his palm, sweating in the day's heat. He could see no point, really, in anyone desiring the death of the old drunk, Depew.

It was the hangman who was stirring up the pot of the Jones murder. Was that reason enough to make him a target? Tree had been shot at before with less reason.

For a long, dragging minute or two, the man in black waited, head down and listening. The shots — he had decided they had been rifle shots — had ceased, and there was a silence hovering over the house and its surroundings. The stand-off was turning stale.

Any more waiting, Tree decided, and he could be asking to be sneaked up on and surprised. He poked his head above the bullet-slivered sill for another quick look. He immediately spotted movement in the bushes, a violence in the leaves. He raised the six-gun, drew a flash bead, and triggered. The slug hammered into the base of the alder where the gunman hid. The jasper's rifle barked response, but the bullet flew wide.

Tree reared again, leveled the heavy .44, and fired.

The rifleman shot back, missing the hangman's diving form. All was still for another minute. Then Tree heard metal crack on metal, then a string of muttered curses, low and intense.

Tree jumped up, vaulted the windowsill smoothly, and pumped his legs into a pounding run toward the gunman's roost. Unless he missed his guess, the polecat's rifle had jammed — and if he happened to have guessed plumb wrong, the likelihood was that he had done so for the last time. However, no bullets were flying in his direction as he pounded yard after yard, unstopped. He leaped the last small gully, slipped, recovered balance, then plunged head-long into the nest of dense shrubs.

His ears caught the sounds of creaking leather, the jingle of a bit. Then he broke clear from tangled branches, to spot the big man swinging up aboard the angular piebald, reined around viciously at the hangman and spurred hard. The huge black-white bore straight down toward Tree. With no place to flee, the hangman boldly stood his ground.

Over the drumming of the hooves, the hangman, his Colt leveled, triggered and triggered again. At the last second the horse swerved, hurtling past in a racket of noise, a flood of swirling, gritty dust. The rider was bent low above the saddle's bow, lashing with his rein ends. Zack Tree glimpsed a flash of checked shirt, a fringed vest, a hat of deep tobacco brown. A stirrup brushed his chest as he jumped back. Catching his balance, he quickly aimed and fired the Colt.

The bullet plowed the rider's back, punching him from the saddle. In an awkward backward somersault, the man bounced hard into a jutting boulder. He slid to the ground and was still.

Tree doubted the need for more shots, but approached carefully, nevertheless. He stopped to stand over the facedown corpse. His bullet had drilled clear through the rider's torso, exiting the chest. Now the checked shirt bore a huge crimson stain. Tree toed the corpse over, none too gently.

It belonged to a man whom he had tangled with before. At the claim up the gulch. The one called Mel. Griswold's man.

Rebecca Dunmore moved solemnly and slowly about the devastated printing room. Her black mourning dress was cut too full for the work she had to accomplish.

She had spent the midafternoon hours, after settling with the undertaker, engaged in the general straightening of the place. Now the upended tables and chairs were all put right. The spilled type — "pie" in printer's lingo — she had swept into a large pile with a broom. She planned to begin the sorting chore when Jory came by after supper; just now his mother had him chopping kindling.

For the moment, though, the young widow paced the floor and battled tears. Life wasn't supposed to be this hard, she thought bitterly. She felt she could never be completely happy again.

Her morbid thoughts roamed back to Missouri. A thousand years ago, it now seemed. In a burst of emotion, her glance fled again to the framed wedding picture hanging on the wall. There the two of them sat, represented in the brassy tintype; pretty bride, handsome groom. Two years ago they had possessed a future.

Now that future together was ashes, nothing more.

She had only one hope left. To make the *Clarion* — her dear Phil's dream — a successful reality.

Rebecca Dunmore forced herself to straighten her spine, raised her chin, and brushed away a tear. A shake of her head sent blond curls back from her face. She banished self-pity in a bright blaze of resolve.

"Becky, you won't build the *Clarion* this way," she told herself. "Phil would want you to pull yourself together. Not waste energy in idle, vain tears." For the first time since she'd learned that Phil had died, she managed a smile. Those terrible villains weren't going to silence the paper! In honor to Phil's precious memory she, too, would be brave!

And the killers would be caught, also, she was now more than certain. Marshal Wilmer was on the job. Likely *that* was why he'd been absent from the funeral.

And if the official law didn't track the killers down, there was still Zachariah Tree. After she'd gotten to know him, Tree actually wasn't so fearsome as he first appeared to her.

The lone woman drew up with a start. The sun-flung rays through the open doorway of the print shop suddenly were blocked. A long, grotesque shadow was thrown on the floor.

Stifling a shriek of fright, she spun to face the newcomer. Almost filling the narrow jambs stood an older man, balding, pink-faced, stout. I know him from somewhere, her racing brain told her. Now, to place the fellow — "Why, you're Mr. Griswold! Cherry Creek Sam!"

"Well, so I am." Griswold's voice was modulated, polite, careful. The man advanced from the entrance and doffed his hat. No longer in silhouette, his form was now clear to the woman. He was well-dressed: broadcloth coat, fancy waistcoat.

"Well, Mr. Griswold, what do you want?" She didn't trust him. There was the link Tree had mentioned between this man and the deaths of Chen and Fong. The item had been in last evening's paper, too recently for her to forget.

Perhaps he had come to question it.

"I want . . . to express my condolences. Yeah, little lady. Sorrow for your man's untimely death." He wagged his round moon head. "Life can get hard, I reckon the lesson shows. A man in his prime, just snatched away. Leaving a gal to grieve."

"I assure you, I'll make out all right."

Griswold's glance roamed the room, hawk-like. The thick, slack lips seemed almost to smack. "Oh? Left you much, did your husband? Never appeared to have much. Just this broke-down printing junk."

"The *Clarion* will be out again soon."

"To print fine lies."

Rebecca Dunmore gasped. The visitor's face had turned hard, cruel — and now he stood over her. She smelled his rank, moist sweat. But she rallied: "Phil's articles were accurate as might be. What he discovered, he printed. And let the chips fall where they may!"

His brow folded in a frown. "Maybe they did fall. Maybe they fell on him. Heavy weight, chips. Can sometimes kill."

"What are you hinting at? That you — "

Then his paunch no longer pressed near her, and his plump face was all wreathed in smiles. "I've hinted at nothing, ma'am. Nothing at all. Miz Dunmore, let me come to the point. Maybe I was riled some when I read the *Clarion* story 'bout me. Felt my business is my business, not the whole town's. What gold claims I might own, my onetime friendship with a Mr. Jones. Why, next thing, I could be accused of unfriendliness. Watering whiskey. Running women of ill fame."

"But all Deadwood knows the place Lil's — "

"Wait!" The man held up his hand. "Don't let's get off the subject, Miz Dunmore . . . Rebecca. I'm here to help, y' see. I feller like me can help a gal like you. A right pretty widow."

A chill crept up the woman's spine. She felt her skin turn to goose bumps. "Mr. Griswold, I don't believe — "

"Here's the proposition. Somebody done in your man, and that puts you on your own. Widows, like everybody, they got to eat, keep dry, wear clothes. You got no chance in Deadwood, and no chance of getting out. Where'd you be going, now without money?"

"I mean to — "

"Hush! There could be some folks think you shouldn't leave. How 'bout them gunnysackers that done for your man? Mighta done for you. Still could. But a female, *in her place*, she's safe."

Fear had nearly broken Rebecca Dunmore's spirit. She hid her hands in her dress folds now to hide their hard trembling. But she tried to keep a bold and nervy front. "And just what, sir, do you find a female's place to be?"

"For sure, not no play at newspapering! A gal's place is in a bed! I'll be blunt, Becky. In a bed *on her back*!

"No!"

"Listen! Come, work at Lil's! It's the only chance you got!" Griswold's eyes turned to diamond-bright slits. "Look right fine in red velvet! You can start tonight!"

"Oh!" she squealed. "Let go my arm!"

In his excitement, he had grabbed her. "We can go over to Lil's right now — "

"Hey! Leave Miz Dunmore be, you!"

They both swiveled their heads. There in the doorway stood the young printer's devil, Jory, his saucerlike eyes wide in childish anger.

"Go 'way, kid!"

"Miz Dunmore, I'll run fetch my ma!" And the boy turned and skedaddled.

"He'll be back," Rebecca warned.

"I reckon he will. But I'm leaving for a spell too. And if you tell what's been said here, I'll claim it's lies. Like the damn paper's trying to ruin me!"

"You — " she spit out. "You — "

He was in the doorway, but he turned to throw a wink. "Don't you cross me, lady. I'll have that li'l old red dress waiting!"

Then he vanished and let in rays of the magenta setting sun.

"So the dead man's up in the brush," Tree was telling the marshal, but Mike Wilmer looked bored. The dusk that had fallen outside made the jailhouse office seem gloomy.

The badge toter's tone was gloomy, too. "Another no-account drifter. Robbery try."

"That's the notion you're buying?"

"What's my other choice? Murder? Who'd want the old judge dead?"

The hangman shrugged. "Well, you heard my story. Now the job's the undertaker's. I done my part."

Wilmer uncoiled from his chair. "Just happened by Depew's place, you did, I reckon?"

"Visit."

"Visit. Uh-uh. Be around town later, Tree? In case of questions?"

"Later. Right now I'm about to take me a ride."

He strode down the jailhouse steps, and viewed the gallows yet another time as he bypassed it. Within a minute Tree was at Garth Henderson's assaying office. Since the door was latched, he gave three rapid knocks.

"Just a second."

"Take your time."

Tree had uttered the words in politeness, but the assayer dawdled till impatience grew big in the hangman's brain. When at last the door swung open, though, it was to a man fully dressed, hair combed down, and neat. "I was rustling up a bite of supper."

"Rustling?"

"Actually, finishing up. Mr. Tree, can I offer you some coffee?"

"If we can drink it on the run and go."

"In a hurry? Man, what's up?"

"I want to take you out to a mine, gather rock samples, and bring them back for you to test as ore."

"At night?"

"Could be that time is running out."

"You want me along?"

"These samples got to be fair ones. The taking done c'rect so's to judge the value of the mine. Now, after dark, could be the only chance that's given. And since I aim to save some lives, I want you in this, Henderson."

The assayer, forgetting his neat part, ran his strong, blunt fingers through the thick, dark shock of hair. "I don't understand. Save lives?"

"Plenty have been lost already. Mining men and others. Plus, you'll get paid for your time."

"It's an unusual request, but I'll go. I'll pack candles and a few tools, and saddle the mare I keep out back."

"I'll go and bring up the bronc I'll be riding myself. Meet you at your gate in ten minutes."

The assayer grinned. "Nighttime breath of air. Might be stimulating. You're persuasive, Tree, I'll have to admit that. What horse shall I be on the lookout for?"

"I'll be forking a rawboned piebald."

"In ten minutes, then. I'll be seeing you."

# Chapter Fifteen

They rode under a murky sky up the Deadwood Gulch trail north, the piebald moving at a strong and smooth trot, Garth Henderson's scrubby roan giving its straddler a jolting time in his nearly worn-out saddle. Passing the cutoff to the Chinese miners' small ravine. It took nearly an hour to reach the wide swing around the prominent rock loaf, another quarter hour to traverse the last up-grade mile. When the landmark outcrop blocked the stars, Tree signaled and both men pulled up.

"This it?"

"Nope, but we'll hike the rest of the way." The hangman reined to the right and into the boulder nest he had used before. "Picket the broncs here. No water and not much graze, but that's

133

just too bad. The gulch ain't exactly livestock heaven."

"Nor much pleasure for people, either," declared the assayer.

"I do reckon we agree on that." Tree helped his sidekick on this mission to transfer the saddlebags from horses' backs to human shoulders. When both men were laden, he led the way to the familiar detritus slope, now a moon-washed sheet of ghostly silver.

It wasn't easy to move quietly, but they did their best. When they topped the first ridge, Henderson paused to catch his breath and survey the route by which they had come. "Pretty steep," the assayer observed.

"And it'll only get steeper. Come on. I'll be signaling when we get ourselves near danger."

"Danger?" In the moonlight Henderson looked blanched. "You aren't serious? I know what you said back down the road, but — "

Tree hurried to reassure the tenderfoot. "I don't really reckon bullets'll start flying tonight, not if things go as smooth as planned, and I'll be in the lead, anyways. But it ain't fair to let you walk into a surprise, and a mine at nighttime can be full of them. Especially if the owner is edgy."

"But I thought *you* — "

"Maybe I led you on some before, but now here's the truth. We're climbing the ridge that's behind the Chinamen's claim, Chen's and Fong's. You recall them two, I reckon. Near all of Deadwood turned out for their hanging."

"That's where I heard the name Tree before! You — Why, sure, you were the hangman brought in — "

"Maybe to my shame, yeah, I jerked the gallows lever. But there's evidence turned up since that the pair mightn't have been guilty, after all. And though the marshal don't pay no mind, I happen to. You see, Henderson, the claims office says there was never doubt about this discovery hole's ownership. A feller name of Griswold has the papers. Alonzo Jones, who salted the claim that's said to be worthless, collected payment from the Chinese suckers, and the money that was paid plumb disappeared. Jones turned up dead, cut to ribbons with a funny-bladed knife — Chinese. But that don't mean Chen and Fong done it, mad at getting cheated or no. Jones himself had just that kind of knife."

"It's pretty complicated," Henderson said. "I didn't follow the case closely at the time. Was buried in my work. The assayer who testified was Sid Doggett, I know. Come to think of it, *he* recently passed away, too. Food poisoning, as I recall."

"It gets better and better, don't it? Add the killing of Phil Dunmore of the *Clarion*, and — well, a blind man can see the drift."

"I heard Dunmore was beaten by masked thugs. Over the paper's defense of *all* Chinese, a touchy subject."

The hangman shifted the shoulder-galling saddlebag, and shrugged. "Don't know for sure. Nobody does — yet. Maybe after tonight."

Conversation flagged, and the men climbed onward and upward, both working up sweats. Finally they topped the last ridge crest and started on down.

"Look here, Tree, I don't see — "

The hangman hushed him with a wave. Both men halted behind a screening clump of pinyons to crouch and wait.

There were no night sounds, no birds, no small animals.

"The claim's below," Zack Tree hissed. "D'rectly below. There's the marker pile of stones over there. The tunnel mouth is beyond." "Nobody's on guard?"

"Oh, someone is, right enough. See the quirly's red glow?"

"What now?" Henderson wanted to know.

"I'll go down. You wait up here, safe. It ain't your fight, this Griswold business, and I'm bound that you don't get hurt." Tree let down the saddlebag and its weight of tools, tested the footing with a toe, and started his descent.

The minutes passed slowly, but the hangman wouldn't be rushed. He kept one eye on the flickering cigarette of the man who watched the claim. The other eye was on the pathless, shifting talus. One false, noisy step, and the jasper would be warned.

He eased the .44 Colt from the holster on his hip, but didn't cock the weapon. Even the softest hammer's click could attract a load of double-aught his way.

Just then a small creature scuttled in the hangman's path, squeaking and scratching the rough rock surface with frantically churning claws. Tree heaved up so as not to stomp on it and worsen things.

But his footing gave way. He slipped and started sliding. The next second a full-blown miniature avalanche was under way, complete with clatter and the bounding of loose stone chunks. Some of the rocks dislodged struck the flat near the guard's position, and the man jumped up.

"Who the hell's there?"

A terrific bang rang out, accompanied by a yard-long spear of flame. Tree felt a gush of wind as the shotgun's charge whizzed past, and he threw himself down heavily, expecting a second triggering. The blast came, but again missed. Seizing his chance while the men were reloading, Tree jumped on the dark adversary. The stock of the Greener glanced off the hangman's skull, but he countered with a Colt-barrel blow, swung blindly.

A yell of pain coincided with the crisp crack of breaking cartilege.

Direct nose hits were always effective. The claim guard staggered back, dropping the clubbed double barrel.

"You son of a bitch!"

The hangman simply waded in again, flailing. His pistol barrel collided with collarbone, jawline, ear, and in a final slash, a mouth. There was the sickening sound of crunching teeth in the darkness. The hurt jasper was down on the flinty ground, writhing.

Zachariah Tree lashed out one more time, this time with his boot. His boot toe impacted the temple, and the man went slack, flopped flat, and lay prone on the earth heap in a motionless lump.

"All clear, Henderson!" Tree shouted into the darkness.

"Shall I come down now?"

"I'd rather that than you fall asleep!"

In a flurry of falling, rebounding gravel, the assayer scrambled to join the hangman. Now the pair stood at the yawning black maw that was the mine's timbered entrance. Henderson let down the armload of bags and began rooting around in them. Tree thumbnailed a lucifer for light.

"Do I need to make this fast?" The hangman touched the match flame to a candle stub. "This here feller'll stay put. I'll just hogtie him."

When the unconscious gunsel's wrists and ankles were snubbed, Tree let himself be handed a small rock hammer. Henderson led the way into the tunnel, holding the candle high, scanning about. Just a few feet within, the men might have been in the deepest mountain's depths for all the clammy, shut-in feeling produced by stagnant air. Tree stumbled on a rough spot in the floor and came close to dropping his specimen bag.

"Watch your step."

"You won't be needing to tell me again."

The expedition proceeded. The tunnel curved, poorly shored up as it was, the way tunnels did in the following of productive veins. But of course, this mine wasn't supposed to be productive. That was the reason why Chen and Fong were supposed to have murdered Jones. It was the reason they were supposed to have sought a bloody revenge. Then Tree and Henderson came to the end of the timbered passage.

But the digging had gone on.

"This appears to have been worked recently," the assayer observed. He moved cautiously forward, squinting.

"How recent?"

"Oh, maybe earlier today?"

The hangman shrugged. "When and where do we start taking up our samples?"

"Here and now.' Garth Henderson suited action to his words by pounding and clinking with his rock hammer. He worked at the sides of the cavern, the ceiling, and most energetically at the head. Soon ore fragments littered the floor, some of them glinting in the soft candlelight.

"What you finding?"

"Seems to be promising quartz."

"Seems to be?" the hangman queried.

"Won't be able to tell for sure till the testing back in the office. But as I said, this galena rock, the formations here, it all looks favorable. This is the claim that Chen and Fong occupied?"

"Certain."

"Strange as hell. Here, help me load these rocks."

The hangman worked quickly and with both hands, as did the assayer. The candles sat perched on tiny outcroppings. Potential nuggets sparked and flashed as they dropped into the bags. "Fool's gold, iron pyrite, do you reckon, Henderson?"

"That could very well be.

They worked awhile longer until Henderson seemed satisfied. "This number of rock chunks should be plenty."

"You're the boss on that score, Henderson."

The pair emerged into star shine, and the air outside the tunnel smelled heavenly with wildflower blossoms. They heard the heavy breathing of the hogtied guard.

"Don't worry," Tree said to the assayer. "He ain't woke up yet, but he's breathing strong. We'll leave him tied. He'll be found in the morning, unless I miss my guess."

"Morning's a good while off."

The hangman shrugged. "Lead a crooked life, you're bound to suffer some."

Making their way back to the horses, the men sweated even harder than they had on the long tramp up because of their heavy load of samples.

Zack Tree and Henderson caught sight of Deadwood a good deal sooner than expected: from a high point on the gulch trail, still at least two miles from boomtown's edge. The hangman was first to note the strange brightness in the sky to the south, and called attention to it.

"Look."

"I see it, Tree. Above the sawtooth ridgeline, that broad red glow. It doesn't look natural."

"Fire is a natural enough thing, ain't it, Mr. Assayer?"

"I've seen forest fires by night before, and they make this peculiar light familiar like."

"But most of the heavy timber close to town's been long cut down for cabins, shorings. Unless you mean — ?"

"Henderson, you're catching my drift. It's got to be buildings, and a passel of them to make that kind of show."

"Damned if you ain't right!"

"We'd best get there, then. No telling just what's happening. By God, man, let's ride!"

He gave hard spur to the piebald's sleek flanks, and the gelding jumped ahead as if shot from a cannon. The hangman heard Henderson's mount on his own mount's fleet heels as both barreled along the trail. Riding this fast over night roads was a risk. In his time in the boom camp he had seen no fire-fighting equipment at all. Certainly Deadwood held no pumping engine to bring water up from a creek.

What he had seen in his day was a burned-out Nevada town. The place had been left little more than a heap of ashes.

"Run, horse, run!"

Rebecca Dunmore was in Deadwood, as well as a few more decent folk. Not everybody was a gunsel or gambler or worse. Not everybody merited a death by rapid, seething flames. The riders burst up the last grade and saw the creek bridge bathed in bright orange light. The blaze was centered off to the left, on the flat that held the poorer-class shanty district. And a goodly part of that dismal area comprised Chinatown.

The neighborhood was ringed by blazing brush and structures.

Although the main part of the town of Deadwood, up beyond, appeared untouched, Chinatown exploded in panic.

A bolting burro splashed through the stream, whinnying in terror.

Zack Tree and Henderson reined up on the grade that approached the bridge.

"What next?"

"You," the hangman directed. "You, Henderson, get yourself on down to your place. You wouldn't be much help around the trouble spot. Best get on with the assay of the samples. Me, I'll just ride on in there."

"To accomplish what?"

"Maybe save some lives — mostly Chinese, I reckon."

"From white townsmen with torches, you mean? There've been threats circulating for weeks."

"Right! I'll meet you back at your office."

However, feisty assayer, features frozen grimly, eyes flashing, was reining the roan down off the main trail and toward the swale. "To hell with keeping me in the clear, Tree! I can do my part!" Almost immediately, the man and horse were lost in a screen of blowing smoke.

Tree urged his own mount in pursuit, the spooked animal balking, but only to be raked harder by the hangman's long-roweled spurs. It was impossible to see. It was impossible not to cough. The smoke was dense, acrid, and ash laden. "Henderson! Hold on! We'll ride together!"

There was no answer but the crackling roar of the blaze. The assayer held the lead and had most likely even increased it. "Damn-fool hot-head!" Tree hacked into the bandanna he now held to his face.

And then, a mighty tower of flame and a wall of heat barred the hangman's progress. Above the noise of fire came many other noises: an occasional shot, an erupting chorus of fierce, loud shouts.

"Damn it, bronc, won't catch him with the way blocked. Got to take the long way 'round!"

He reined down along the creek's bank and gave hard spur.

# Chapter Sixteen

The miner with the rolled-up sleeves and monstrous arms had mounted the railed porch of Lil's Place with a yell and a bound. He had brandished an ax handle of stout hickory wood, and the eyes of the throng he had attracted fixed him in the red light of the doorway lamp. "Been wrestlin' the damned *arrastra* box all week, me'n m' pard!" the man shouted. "Got us ten, twenty dollars' worth o' dust, and it's gone for bacon and beans! Low gold pickings and sky-high prices! The prospect holes gone barren, by God! And there's no fresh ground for to be staked!"

A roar from the crowd. The crowd had turned to a seething human mass, and the mood gone ugly.

"We hears you, Jake!"

"Chinks holdin' too much good ground!"

"Goddamn shame!"

The man called Jake raised his voice again. "Asked for a job, but the cafe man had hired him a coolie! Coolies in eatin' places, coolies in laundries!"

"Th' slant-eyed heathen in the streets and in the stores," someone called.

"They're now ever' where, b' God!"

"Ever' where, and damn it, it do gall!"

Across the way, a would-be gunslinger clung to a store-porch post. His rusty beard bristled, his mouth formed a gap-toothed O. "The rat-soup eaters, they save all the gold they make!"

A tinhorn in striped pants squealed: "*Our* gold! *Our* money!"

"White man's goddamn land!"

The fury of the street throng had been burgeoning. Now, the ranks swelled the entire length of saloon row. Twenty establishments were at that moment disgorging rowdy, drunken men. They stamped deep dust underfoot as they milled. Some flourished bottles. Some swilled greedily from hefty jugs.

"Yeah, white man's land, white man's gold property," whooped a miner in bib overalls.

"*We* dug it, chopped down trees!"

"Drove the injuns out!"

"So then, who benefits? Goddamn coolies?"

"No, damn it to hell!"

"No, *no* , *no* !"

That was the way it had all started. The saloon area was filled boardwalk to boardwalk with men. Shops emptied, and whores lay neglected in their cribs. On the balcony of the fine Dakota House, a feed-shop clerk called angrily, "What we gonna do! Sit and take it?"

A miner below roared, "Drive the coolies out! Stomp their asses! Burn their shanties down! *Burn 'em*, I say!"

Lanterns had appeared in enraged men's hands. Pine-knot torches were set alight with lucifers.

And the whole mob started its swift, short march. Short, because the Chinatown at the edge of Deadwood wasn't far. Swift, since it was reached in minutes, and without warning. Hordes of miners, gunsels, and roughnecks poured down the gullies; their brush had been cleared, and the shrubs were turned into kindling for cooking.

Even the paths between the shacks were neatly swept.

From the foot of Main Street, Mike Wilmer watched the human flow with interest. "What d' you know," he growled to his current woman, a full-hipped Swede endowed with enormous breasts. "Here's a troublin' as don't concern me, for once."

"But, honey, you're the marshal, no?" Helga questioned.

He quieted her by hustling her toward his rented room.

In the backmost crib in Lil's, Brace Haldane fell atop his partner. She was a wispy girl of four feet ten. He was a treetop, by far the tallest man in town. "Ain't you going to join the mob, big feller?" she asked, hoping.

"Naw. Let the feisty dogs kill the mangy coolie rats!"

He entered the woman quickly and brutally. Her harsh shriek was lost in the cheers ringing outside. The mob had torched the first Chinese structure, a slab-board joss house. The ideograph sign flamed up brilliantly, and the miners clamored. "*More* !"

The hairy-armed man drove his ax handle into a small Chinese man's solar plexus. The youth in tight striped pants yanked a fleeing fellow's queue and pulled him into a vicious face punch. Two burly mule skinners trapped an old Chinaman with a wisp of beard and clubbed him to the earth with fists.

A Chinese youth, scarcely out of his teens, was tripped, ganged up on, and kicked by a dozen mud-caked boots. The kid raised a piercing wail till it was cut off by a wheel spoke rammed into his quivering lips.

The cry, "We done got the coolies on the run!" rang between the tumbledown shanties.

"Grab the heathen!"

"String 'em up and whip their yeller hides!"

"Yeah, stretch their goddamn necks!"

Chinatown was a maze of short streets fanning out among low hills. Erosion-scarred alleys snaked and zigzagged, mostly less than a block in length, and dead-ending against steep gulch walls. The mob of white men stormed through the shanty town, with fire in their hands. Torches multiplied and were passed around.

A placer man tossed a blazing pine knot onto a shanty's roof. The structure went up like an ignited paper lantern. The blaze spread rapidly to three adjacent dwellings, and all exploded in a mass of flame.

Frightened men with queues fled in all directions. Some were shot, some were dragged down with pickax-hardened miners' hands. Some screamed, some were given no chance to scream. Some were cut with knives and left to bleed.

Crackling flames leaped up tinder-dry and fragile buildings. Roofs collapsed in showers of sparks. Walls toppled, crushing men and animals. The smoke that billowed heavenward was thick and black, and blotted the moon and stars. In the chaos of yells and shrieks, leaders emerged, leaders vicious and tough and cruel. One was a bearded gunsel. "Tie this 'un's hands to that tree! Hoist 'im . . . thataway! Now for the mule skinner's whip. Lay her on, Jack! Stripe the yeller back! Stripe it!"

The pinioned Chinaman flopped like a gaffed carp.

Then another man with his arms lashed together was drawn high. Clawing fingers stripped the scrawny frame. His papery skin was stretched as tight as a drumhead over his torso's fragile rack of bones. The blacksnake whip popped and snapped and laid on finger-thick welts. The skin split and parted to show white bone. Blood welled, trickled, then flowed.

The sky also glowed orange-red below the coils of pumping smoke. The crackling of the fire had become a roar, assaulting and exciting the ears. Singsong cries in the Chinese language were quelled with clubs and fists. Shiny faces that looked polished were battered mercilessly. "Stop 'em! Don't let 'em run!"

Then a furious giant with a beard the color of ripe wheat strode up the alley, a squalling, struggling Chinaman under either massive arm. Both the prisoners were drenched and streaming. At a juncture of lanes he hurled his victims in the dirt. "These two!"

Rampant whites crowded around in a close knot. "Jocko, lad!"

"Look, boys, it's Mad Jack O'Toole!"

"Ain't nobody hates the furriners worse!" Mad Jack O'Toole scowled. "Lynch the goddamn uppity scum! Who's got a good, strong rope?"

The mob milled a minute as confusion reigned. Then someone offered: "Found some in a hut! Here's a new hemp coil!"

"Haul the heathen to the crossbeam over that there Chink house."

It was the work of only minutes to tie crude noose knots, and draw the loops tight around two pulsing, frightened throats. The crossbeam stood wide and high off the ground, with a good many limbs low-sprouting and available. Mad Jack's friends dragged additional victims near, lashed their hands like those of the others, and

149

shoved them to the fore. At last four unfortunate Chinese stood in a ragtag row; the first man with a rope noosed about his neck trembled in frayed cloth slippers, moaning.

Jack assumed the role of master of ceremonies.

"Ready?" yelled Mad Jack O'Toole in a half-crazed bellow. "I'm countin' three, and then you'll haul like hell, you end-handlin' fellers! One! Two! And — "

"Wait!"

Into the firelit area near the cottonwood's base raced a rawboned roan horse flecked with sweat. From the saddle swung a man wearing a candystripe shirt. He waved his spindly arms and shouted, "Citizens of Deadwood, you can't!"

"Grab the loco son of a bitch!" yelled a gruff-voiced miner.

Garth Henderson was clutched by a dozen pairs of hands. Although he twisted and fought, he was pulled back roughly, and had his arms pinned to his sides by arms three times as strong.

Mad Jack O'Toole thrust his face close to the assayer's. "What your ass doin' down in Chinatown, feller?"

"I'm glad I got here when I did! I saw the flames, guessed a tragedy was in the making." He gestured with a shake of the head. "And it appears it's all intentional! And you're about to string up my laundryman there! Lee Chung!"

Mad Jack struck him then, the knuckles of his callused hand meeting the soft flesh of the

150

pinned man's midsection. "Ugh!" Henderson bent at the middle like a patent hinge.

"Chung, huh? I'll 'Chung' you, you — "

A pained gasp. An agitated wheeze. "The Chinaman's a good fellow! A worthy member of the community — "

"Keep your mouth shut, tenderfoot. In a minute he'll be another monkey dancin' on a rope."

"No!"

"Okay, boys, jerk that rope!"

And the miners, all powerfully muscled men, bent their bulging shoulders to the task and dragged the victim from the ground. There would be no swift neck-snapping drop now; only the steady and slow pull, the cruelest, most agonizing of executions. Chung's face turned a deathly bluish purple. His almond eyes grew as round as fried eggs, and almost as glossy. And those eyes continued to swell and bulge. Through contorting lips, a hideous black tongue popped. Legs kicked and thrashed convulsively.

Death's slow march was played with the utmost pain. Mad Jack crowed, and Garth Henderson strained against the burly men who held him. Again and again he tried to turn his head, but found it forced back to view the ghastly tableau. The twitching, bucking, horror-filled neck stretching dragged on. Minutes turned to a quarter hour of gurgling squelch sounds.

At last the victim's twitching lessened, and finally ceased. Against the backdrop of the blazing Chinatown swung one corpse, his neck twice its normal length. Even the twisting energy of the rope had been exhausted.

Thrill-seeking roughnecks cast their eyes to the other Chinamen waiting in line.

"Turn the tenderfoot loose. Send 'im home to ma!" But when Henderson's arms were freed, the outraged assayer chose to launch himself at O'Toole.

Mad Jack's bunched fist drove to the assayer's jaw, and the smaller man fell back. "So he wants a fight on his puny hands, now, does he? Stand aside, gents, whilst I teach the son of a bitch a lesson."

A shot rang out. The big miner grunted and clutched his chest, then pitched facedown and flat in the trampled dirt. The shot man kicked out twice, and was still.

"Who's next?"

More than a dozen heads swung as one. "Gawd," gasped one onlooker.

"Who it be, Joe?"

"Why, it's the goddamned hangman feller!"

"Killed Jack dead!"

"Let's carve the bastard's fuckin' eyes out!"

The gunsel with the red beard palmed an Arkansas toothpick a foot in length. He dipped and darted quickly off to Zachariah Tree's right side and as the hangman came around with the Colt, the red-beard dove under the spearing muzzle blast into Tree's legs.

Knocked backward with a staggering force, the hangman went down.

"Hey, Joe! Gutbucket!" The red-bearded jasper yelled. "Give a pard a hand! This one's strong as a goddamned curly wolf!"

The men called Joe and Gutbucket lost no time in jumping into the fray. One assaulted the cornered hangman head on, the other circled him from behind in a titanic bear hug.

Now Tree's gun arm was pinned to his side, and although he clutched the weapon still, he couldn't bring it into play. The pressure applied to his heaving rib cage was like a vise. He battled lancing pain and loss of breath. Wild blood pounding in his brain made things difficult; his vision blurred. One thought alone remained: Don't give up, Zack! Don't give up!

While Joe threw every ounce of strength into squeezing Tree, Gutbucket battered the hangman in front, directing hits to his head and exposed abdomen that felt like sledge blows. Tree slumped perceptibly, throwing his whole weight forward. Joe was dragged along. For a split second, the iron grip was loosened.

Powering up on his legs then, Tree retaliated. A driving kick jammed a boot toe to Joe's knee, caving it in, and the noise was like the cracking of a stomped matchbox. With his gun hand free now, Tree brought the six-gun up to trigger it once, twice, three times. Three men lay dead around him.

"That's the way, hangman!" whooped Garth Henderson. "Drill them! Drill the bastards! Shoot our way clean out of here!"

Tree stepped to Henderson's side. The assayer was down. The hangman dragged him to his feet. "Can you walk?"

"Barely."

"Come on. Let's find the horses."

On one side a collapsing building's roof exploded in a mass of sparks. On their other side, flames furiously leaped skyward, fueled by shanty walls, Chinese possessions, and Chinese clothes.

"Up on the roan's back," Tree commanded, and the limping, pain-wracked assayer managed to obey. Then Tree swung to the piebald's saddle. Both men fisted reins and dug their mounts' flanks with their heels.

They didn't rein the gelding and mare in until they had splashed through the creek.

"Maybe we should turn back, try to help," the assayer opined. His face was soot streaked, scraped, and battered, generally looking like hell.

"Not much point to it. It's about over. The lucky ones lived."

"Those rampaging roughnecks — "

Tree shook his head. "We could shoot a few more. But hating Chinese, it's a damn pastime in this town. We can't wipe all the bastards out alone."

"Then you're riding for town?"

"We're riding for town. Those rock samples we took, they're safe?"

"In the saddlebags."

"They ain't the kind of thing I'm likely to forget," Zack Tree announced seriously. "The damn nuggets could be the key to stop all this killing and put some killers in the place they really belong — at the end of a rope. Then, let's see how brave they act."

The pair rode on into Deadwood in a gloomy silence.

# Chapter Seventeen

Tree watched from the padded rocker beside the desk while the assayer assiduously bent to his task. Henderson was, if anything, a very careful man, and his trained hands handled his tools as smoothly as a practiced surgeon's. "The mix of sulfuric and nitric acid must be . . . there. The grainy dust in the tube . . . then the bicarbonate of soda for the precipitator."

"How much?" the curious hangman queried.

"Unbelievable! Let me try again."

Zack Tree built another quirly and waited for the man to finish.

"My God!

"Damn it, Henderson, spit it out, man! It's getting light outside. Morning's come, and time, it's a-starting to waste!"

"If this calculation is correct, and I'd stake my rep on it . . . well! Those two Chinamen Chen and Fong were squatting on a bonanza! Worth well over six hundred dollars per ton!"

Even though he had expected a rich verdict, the hangman's eyebrows raised. "Then the claim, it would pay off to work it?"

"And following the vein clear to the mountain's center! As I said, Zack, a bonanza! Bring the deep-rock miners on, the steam engines, the pumps! Gigantic stamp mills have been built for far less promising mine property — and paid for themselves a hundredfold!"

"Chen and Fong couldn't have known about it."

"You don't think so?" the assayer asked.

"If you can be a couple of millionaire magnates, do you carve up the man who sold you the mine? No, not even if he'd tried to cheat you when he done it! You'd instead go straight out and shake the damn fool's hand."

Henderson turned from his balance scales and samples, and wiped his dusty hands. "Don't make much sense then that Jones would get killed by the Chinamen."

"The business is about messy as a stable floor." Tree pulled out two gold pieces and handed them to Henderson. "That should about cover it for your time, Henderson. Much obliged for your help." He headed for the door.

"What will happen now?"

"Why, I expect there'll be more hangings in these parts inside another week or two. And

# THE HANGMAN

Deadwood town, Dakota Territory, had best brace for all the hell that's to be raised!"

Mike Wilmer was sleeping particularly well in the bed he rented in the little boardinghouse. Often Black Bear Street, adjacent to saloon row, was not anywhere so quiet, or the center of Deadwood so free of disturbance for an entire night through. Plus, there was the fact of steamy Helga's attentions — welcome anytime, of course, but most welcome when the lawman had no other fish to fry.

Now Wilmer snored in the window's rays of morning sun, his long johns moist with sweat, and Helga, beside him, modest in a sleep-time silky camisole.

From the hall through the door, Tree could hear the man. Using the heel of his hand, he pounded at the door. On the other side, Wilmer and the woman came awake and sat bolt upright. The lawman grabbed his solid old Remington Navy off the bedside chair. Helga snatched a sheet corner to cover her legs.

"Who the hell's there?"

"Tree."

"Tree, the hangman?"

"I got some news of killings and who I reckon had to've done the dirty deeds. A chance to throw a few low bastards in that jailhouse cage of yours, and not innocent men this time, neither."

"This got to do with the ruckus last night? If some Chinamen sparked 'em a passel of trouble, 'taint the law's nevermind, leastways — "

"It ain't last night I'm talking of," Tree called angrily through the door. "It's about the Jones claim."

The unshaven, heavy-jowled man sighed. "Gal, go let him in — whilst I throw some pants on this old hind end. Can't greet a caller in holey balbriggans. 'Tain't fitting."

"Me? And do you want me to wait while you talking?"

"The pretty sight is likely to cheer me up a peck."

Her large breasts swaying heavily under fragile cloth, she unbolted the door and pulled it open.

"Set, Tree," Wilmer said. The man's blunt fingers fumbled clumsily with his shirt buttons. Then came time for polishing his star. The lawman went to work on the gleaming copper with an energetic sleeve.

"I'd just as soon stand," Tree said. " We could be moving out quicklike. Here's what I found out." Wasting few words, speaking coolly and fast, Zachariah Tree unwound a yarn of sample-taking, assay analysis, and mine worth. He proceeded to the duping of a pair of ignorant Chinese men, and of sly trickery backfiring on the wrong doer. The hangman concluded by telling of a murder with the blame put on a goat.

"And so, Chen and Fong likely didn't even own the murder knife," he concluded. "Alonzo Jones had him a couple of the kind stashed with his possibles. You can ask the Conway woman, marshal."

"Nell Conway?"

The hangman nodded.

"She's a low-down one-dollar whore!"

Tree took a glance at Helga, where she sat on the straw tick. The raw language didn't affect her a bit. She gnawed away at a chipped fingernail.

"The Conway woman's a witness."

"Witness to what?" Wilmer scowled irritably. "And this Garth Henderson. Sure, the feller's an assayer, but with an axe to grind, most likely, for to soften up his customers. And if them ore samples was got hold of illegal-like — "

"Marshal, *murder* is illegal. Murder of Jones, murder of Depew, and biggest shame of all, murder of newspaperman Phil Dunmore. And my own face is more than a little red, I'm willing to confess. I hanged a pair as were innocent as turtles on a log. And admit something yourself, Wilmer: the damned real killers had you buffaloed, too. Was I you — "

"Hangman Tree, get something straight. You ain't me, and you ain't official law in Deadwood, neither! Not by a damn sight. I got some advice, and it's this. Your work, it's done with. Take yourself and your case of ropes and hangman's gear, and clear on out of town!"

The iron gray eyes had gone hard at the marshal's words. "You're an ornery feller, Wil-

mer. Ornerier than I'd have reckoned. Most lawmen would be — "

"I ain't most lawmen, am I, Helga?"

The woman, eyes downcast, murmured, "No."

"Nor anything like, by God! So, Tree, you goin'
to ride on out on this morning's stage?"

Tree's voice was now steely edged. "Hadn't
planned on it, no. Got some cleaning up to do."

"Best be doin' it at the bathhouse."

The hangman was in the doorway by this
time. His face was hard as a granite tombstone
slab. His big right hand hovered three inches
above the big Colt gun. "You won't find me at a
bathhouse, because I ain't dirty, Wilmer. Not like
some folks in this town of yours. Not even like
its head star packer."

The flab-fleshed marshal said nothing. His
woman was statue still, statue quiet as Tree
walked out.

Back out in the main street, in the shadow of the
gallows, Tree encountered the young widow. He
saw Rebecca Dunmore emerging from the
greengrocer's shop, a woven basket under her
arm that indicated she had been shopping.
Above the shiny black dress her face looked
pale, and her blond hair was tucked into a bun.
Very proper. Very prim.

"Oh, Mr. Tree," she said, surprised. "Zack. I'm
glad you happened along. Oh! Your face! Were
you in a fight?" Her expression was suddenly all
concern.

"You might call it that. Listen, Rebecca, some things have happened since I seen you last, some things that concern Phil's killer and the bad actors that attacked you. There's sure as the devil more on our plate than the hatred for Chinese folks in this town. Phil wasn't beat up on no account but that the *Clarion* attacked Sam Griswold."

"My God!"

He took the woman's black-clad elbow and guided her to the boardwalk's edge. Most passersby took little notice of the pair.

"I can't take a lot of time to jaw with you just now," the hangman told her. "But you should know, I reckon, that the key goes clear back to Jones's murder. There Cherry Creek Sam had him the strongest reason for wanting his sidekick dead. Yeah, him and old Alonzo had been in cahoots. And it was when I started to catch on, that I started to draw sneak bushwhacks on me — *and* folks I happened to get near. Even old Enos Depew took a bullet with my name on it."

"I'd heard the judge had been shot and killed. And listen, Zack? I'm sure you're right about Griswold and his schemes. It all makes sense. Do you know, he approached me yesterday and made the most vile offer? To go work for him in his . . . in his . . ."

"The son of a bitch's parlor house? Well, just something else that he'll soon be paying for. I'm on my way over to the place called Lil's now."

"Aren't you bringing the marshal in?"

The hangman shook his head. "That's another story. But I've handled men as bad as Griswold and his bunch before. I'll just do it again. And I aim to catch the old weasel at his breakfast in his den."

"Won't his bodyguards be there swarming?"

Zack Tree shrugged. "Somebody's got to go after Cherry Creek Sam. If I act quick enough, I can surprise him and get the drop. Grab the leader, the pack'll go hightailing. It's true with sheep and Indians. He threw her a lopsided smile.

"Just be careful, Zack."

He left her in front of the nearly completed new bank building and crossed the street, dodging among the freight wagons and teams, the trains of pack mules, the horseback riders both male and female who saw fit to be up and about so early. His Waterbury watch called the morning hour a few minutes shy of nine. On the boardwalk passing the livery stable, he waved to Dan. The brawny kid shook his dung-caked pitchfork and grinned. Tree strode straight past, and in a dozen or so more yards, was in the midst of saloon row.

He moved a bit more rapidly now, the sun heating up as it climbed the sky. He passed the loafers that lounged against the hitching rails, and he passed the strolling women — not a few of them whores.

He finally made it to Lil's, Cherry Creek Sam Griswold's headquarters. The slimy den of thieves, crooked politicians, throat-cutters.

# THE HANGMAN

Tree paused a moment just outside of the bat-wings and exhaled slowly, then pushed through and on under the sagging canvas roof. Not much longer now. Not much longer, at all. He cast his gaze about.

At the early hour, Olive was nowhere about. There seemed to be no one to greet him on the cheap, plushy premises; no females of any duty, not even cleaning women.

And no men.

Tree could hear the street sounds drifting in: the creak of wheels, the straining leather. Now and then, a lusty drover gave a shout.

No sounds coming from the cribs, either.

The hangman's thoughts raced. Could be that Griswold was in his private room. Could be that so were his boyo crew of gunsels. Could be Brace Haldane.

Haldane spelled trouble at any place and at any time. Bad trouble. Gun trouble, and the big bastard wore two of them, not counting holdout derringers in his pockets and sleeves.

"Griswold! Hey, Griswold! You got you a visitor! Answer up, I know you're here!"

A low, gruff voice drifted, muffled, through the familiar inner panel. "Tree, that you? Hike on back. Push on open my damned office door."

Zack Tree ambled easily across the floor and did so, then crossed the threshold and faced the boss crook's hard, cold stare.

# Chapter Eighteen

Tree's eyes darted as quickly as a chuckwalla's tongue around the shabby, crowded room. Griswold sat alone at the table, this time with an open ledger, inkwell, and pen neatly spread before him. Then the parlor house owner fixed his visitor with a phony smile.

He did not appear a man with a guilty conscience. But the hangman had dealt before with jaspers able to run a bluff.

"Well, Mr. Tree, I see you're out and about right early." Griswold's voice was about as cool as pond ice, the same temperature as his squinting, coal-dark eyes.

"They do claim that it's the early bird as catches the worm," the hangman responded. "But that's just an old adage. I don't figure you for a worm, Griswold — though you're plenty low enough for a snake."

Griswold shifted his bulk in the big chair with the cane-wove seat. "Just say what you come to say."

"You heard about the riot last night? A white mob burned down Chinatown? Some harmless foreigners that weren't guilty of a damned thing, they got lynched?"

"Word's around Deadwood on it." Griswold shrugged. "None of my affair what miner trash do."

"Right nice way to talk about your own men like that." Griswold's jaw set.

"Men from right here at Lil's. Like Carl, the feller with the reddish chin brush? I had to put a bullet in him last night. Another hardcase some called Gutbucket —"

"Joe."

"Yeah, Joe." The hangman raised an eyebrow. "I was told the boys got shot up. Didn't hear by who. Now I know."

"Any way you cut it, Griswold, today you come up shy of hired guns. Mighty shy. Especially since you lost another one killed yesterday. I mean the one that tried to pick me off, but missed and took out Judge Depew."

"I don't know what you're talking about."

"At this point, my story gets plumb interesting. The man I killed up by Depew's house, he was out at your gold claim just this week, looking hard and talking tough to fellers like me who came around curious. You ain't forgot your gold claim, have you? The one up the Gulch, once was worked by Chen and Fong? Property got sold to them by Alonzo Jones. For sure, you ain't forgot Jones."

Cherry Creek Sam Griswold leaned well back, did not smile, and did not frown. But he did gesture expansively with a hand large as a bear paw, although soft as a pillow. "Maybe we do got some things to jaw about, hangman. Have a chair."

Tree continued standing. "I'm listenin'."

"It's a fact I knew Jones. More'n few knew him. He was a loser at near everything he touched." The smooth fingers of the former Denverite dipped into a drawer. Tree held his breath, but Sam Griswold came up holding no more than an oblong cedar box. The stogie was black, a foot long and one inch thick. "You a cigar man, Tree?"

"When the company's right."

"Suit yourself," Griswold said, biting off the tip. He scratched a lucifer and he lit up, watching the hangman over the growing cloud of bitter smoke. "Fact is, Jones owed near every saloon keeper and cardplayer in town."

"Including you."

Griswold nodded. " 'Course, money ain't the only way to make good a marker. Some prefer to work it off."

Tree kept his hand near his Colt. "Like by salting worthless claims and tricking Chinamen?"

"Ain't no secret that when I first came to the Gulch I dug some prospect holes, true. I even staked a claim and filed on it. Found more gold in cribs and rotgut. Plumb forgot I even had it 'til — "

"Jones unloaded it on Chen and Fong on your say-so, and they struck it rich. Jones came crying for his cut with threats to go to the law, so your men killed him and pinned it on the Chinamen, with the help of a judge pickled senseless."

"You do spin a good yarn, Tree. Ever think of writin' dime novels?" Griswold chuckled.

Tree grit his teeth. Griswold seemed a bit too cocky, he thought, for a man without his guards around. He checked the room again, but saw no one.

"Plan would've worked, too, but for Phil Dunmore's murder. Now, that was stupid. Or did the gunnysackers you sent to wreck the *Clarion* office happen to go too far?"

Griswold's face turned hard. "Hangman, *you* just may have gone too far."

"I'm marching you to the jail now, Griswold. You can own up to the marshal, and he'll throw you in the cage, awaiting trial by jury and a sober judge."

"Nothing can be proved." Griswold wasn't stirring.

"Maybe, but when the jury hears your no-account gunsels spill the beans and see the assayer's report of the ore strike worth millions, they'll have proof enough."

The whoremaster rose from his chair. "You son of a bitch, Tree! The plan was airtight! I won't stand for you sticking your damned nose in. Haldane!"

The gunfighter burst through the private rear door, carrying a long-barreled Remington in each fist, his pockmarked face twitching in expectation of gunplay.

But quickly as the gunfighter moved, Zack Tree was quicker. With a pivot and a step, he had grabbed Griswold, and now pressed the .44 to the fat, bald head. "Try it, Brace, and Cherry Creek Sam buys a slug!"

The thin lips of Haldane compressed savagely. "Damn your hide, Tree! Here's — "

Griswold's shattered face was blubbering. "Don't shoot, Haldane!"

The rawboned beanpole of a man had slumped to a crouch, his lanky arms extended, forefingers hooked on triggers and stroking fluidly. Haldane held as still as a brooding statue, waiting a full minute before easing up.

"Looks like you win for now, hangman."

"Throw down your shooting irons."

The tall man did so with a wolfish snarl. The two hand cannons clanked loudly on the warped floorboards.

"Now stand over by the bunk."

This time the gunfighter obeyed also. Tension hung in the room's air, a heavy, chilling force. Zachariah Tree moved a step from the quaking Griswold, and covered both men now.

The hangman permitted himself the smallest of tight smiles. "What the hell's going on, boss?"

Haldane said. The gunfighter's pocked face was downcast, eyes sparking frustrated fire.

"Our hangman friend" — the words were spit out spitefully — "has took him a passel of crazy notions he aims to make stick with ol' Mike Wilmer. Ain't nothing but talk."

Tree held the Peacemaker level, unmoved. "We can all talk till the cows come home, but we'll do it at the jailhouse. Single file, gents, and over by the front door. And if Olive or any of them so much as sneeze, this here .44 barks first at you, Sam."

"Do as he says, Haldane."

The men were lined up, hands raised, ready to trot, when two women tramped through the open door.

"Sorry, Sam," Olive blurted out quickly, "but this widow bitch just marched right back here before I could — " She swallowed her words when she saw the guns.

"Shut up, Olive," Griswold barked. "Get your ass out, now!"

Olive took the hint and ran out.

Tree glanced quickly at the woman in black. "Rebecca, we got business at the jail, so if you'll — "

She moved closer. "Zack, I came here to give Mr. Griswold a piece of my mind."

"Becky, we got to get to these men to the marshal. You can tell them later."

"No, I'll speak my piece now, face-to-face. Griswold, I know the kind of man you are. When you thought me helpless and without recourse, you sought to force me to a life of sin! But I'm no soiled dove, sir, nor could I ever be! You're despicable!"

The angry woman stepped between Zack Tree and Griswold, drew back her hand, and slapped Sam's fat face.

Tree's line of fire obstructed, Haldane saw his chance. The gunfighter's arm snaked out and drew the woman in, jerking her against his hard torso. She squawked briefly like a trapped sage hen, but had her outcry stifled. The lean giant's massive paw closed on her throat, and then nobody moved.

"Tree, now you just toss down that hogleg! Yeah, else I wring the chicken's pretty neck! You, Griswold, grab the bastard's Colt. Grab my Remingtons, too, and hand the sons of bitches to me!" Too Goddamned bad!"

The big man lifted her bodily and shook her. She made no sound, but her limbs flopped about as crazily as a doll's.

"Hurt her, Haldane, and I'll kill you, for sure."

"Oh, hangman? If you ain't dead first, you mean."

Griswold thrust a gun to where Haldane could close on it. The gunsel immediately thumbed the firearm to cock. "Wait," the bald man said. "We got to get away. Shots, they'll fetch a crowd. They always do in Deadwood."

"Livery stable's down the alley, boss. There's broncs in the corral."

"Snag a couple, we'll clear out on 'em. Luck's run out hereabouts. Got to save our necks!"

171

"You're in charge, Griswold. But the gal, she comes along."

Griswold threw open the door to the back alley. "Right. She'll be hot bedroll company out on the trail." Then to Zack Tree he commanded: "Hangman! Back inside, damn you! Keep back inside."

The hangman stepped back while the men forced the woman through the narrow door. But her full petticoats bulged the black dress's skirts to snag on the rough wooden doorjamb.

"Goddammit," Griswold snarled.

Brace Haldane's eyes flicked from the hangman's a split second.

Just enough for Tree to launch a low dive at Haldane's knees. The move was clumsy, but there was no choice. The hangman had no time. But he did have guts.

Haldane sidestepped, and grunted: "Fool!" His gun barrel chopped down in a vicious arc. It connected solidly with the hangman's head, crushing his hat and opening his head.

The last thing he felt was his own hot blood on his face before he blacked out.

# Chapter Nineteen

Zachariah Tree came around groggy and hurting, still facedown in the splinters of the office floor at Lil' s. He was wracked by nausea, his head split from ear to ear. But the hangman managed to roll himself up onto braced elbows, rear his lower body to bring his shaky legs into play, and finally heave himself erect. The first thing he noticed was that he was alone. The next, that his trusty Peacemaker was gone.

His hand dipped to his boot top and groped clumsily for a moment. A weak smile overcame his features. He had palmed the miniature Captain Jack. He breathed silent thanks to Mr. Hopkins and Mr. Allen, the manufacturers of the handy hideout gun. Then Tree retrieved his crushed Stetson and was ready to move.

There was no time to waste. Griswold and the gunfighter had a lead on their way to vacating Deadwood, and they had Rebecca. Once into the badlands with the woman, and their lust sated, the pair weren't the kind to turn her loose alive.

The hangman plunged through the door and out into the back alley. There were no people to be seen, only swarms of flies and several scrawny, yapping curs.

Tree forced his legs into a painful lope, and soon the livery's rambling stable and adjacent corral came into view. From the gate in the propped pole rails, he scanned the area with those cool gray eyes. A great big pen full of unsaddled horses, strangely peaceful. Usually they got a bit skittery after mounts were cut out by the stable hand.

Then his gaze swept the building proper. Working on gut feeling, he headed toward them, the Captain Jack's hammer thumbed and preceding him as he edged to the weathered wall. When he reached the open doorway, he threw himself through, and into a belt of gloomy twilight filled with motes, drifting, hay and stink of horseshit.

A voice pierced the oppressive stillness. "Zack! Oh, thank God you've come! Look here!"

Tree ran immediately toward the voice in the shadows. Becky was hunkering down in the corner, her dress ripped and covered with blood and hay. "You got away from them."

Her tone was tense and very bitter. "'Got away' isn't the term. This boy sacrificed himself to save

174

me." She directed the hangman's glance downward.

"Dan, the stable kid?" He touched the huddled, still form that she crouched over, and his hand came away sticky. Pitchfork tines had ripped the youth's abdomen. The hay was strewn with great gobs of blood and innards.

"Griswold and the other brute, they ran in here after saddles, and of course, with me in tow. The boy challenged them. Then the tall one — ?"

"Haldane."

"Haldane simply laughed. Then he barged ahead. He lashed out with his fist, and the boy, Dan, was clubbed down. But he jumped right back up and tried to fight. He saw me by then, held by the men, all messed and struggling. He did his best."

"I didn' t see the varmints come out the back."

"They ran out through the front, Zack. The stagecoach was standing at the depot."

"Damn!"

A distraught nod. "Haldane driving, yes. Sam Griswold all squeezed up inside."

Tree was already up and charging toward the street. He emerged into a blinding glare and a buzz of angry shouts.

A crowd was knotted up in the street, talking and gesturing to beat the band. A few guns were in some townsmen's hands, but there was no shooting. The gathered folks were staring off up the street west, in the direction of the main route of town.

The townsmen said the road threaded north through canyons and ravines. It also hairpinned a set of cliff faces that would scare a sure-hooved burro.

"Ain't the marshal going after the sons of bitches?" Tree asked no one in particular. "They just gutted Dan in the stable over there!"

A toothless old-timer gummed it out: "Can't nobody find the lawman! Anyways, he'd never lead a posse outta town!"

They were all shopkeepers' wives, old loafers, or sore-backed whores. Not an honest *pistolero* in the pack. The stage jehu had vanished to where the cowards hid — at least Tree was unable to spot him. The hangman pictured the careening coach, and rushed to a decision. "This saddled stallion at the hitch rail," he called out. "I'm borrowing him." He vaulted to the back of the blaze-nosed black brute, reined about, and kicked the animal into a run. It was a powerful quarter-horse stud, heavy haunched and fleet. The mount and rider shot up past saloon row, churning a cloud of yellow dust out of the town and down the rutted, treacherous track.

The stage tooled along briskly behind the running four-hitch of sweating bays. Brace Haldane, tall on the driver's box, leaned far forward and cracked the braided, lead-weighted whip. Haldane had worked as a bullwhacker in his youth, driving teams in the deserts of California, the Mojave and Death Valley. Those days of long-hauling the salty

borax had honed men to such whipcord tough-
ness that would last their lives.

"Jesus Christ," Sam Griswold yelled, his flabby
upper body hanging out from the stage window,
gritting teeth into the dusty wind of passage, and
waving an arm. "This damned road is too narrow for fast driving! It' s a ledge along a goddamned cliff!"

"Take a look along the back trail!" Haldane
called down. "Ain't you seeing the same thing as
me?"

"Plume of dust! Posse!"

Haldane nodded and shook his reins, and
snapped the whip harder and louder beside the
surging animals' ears. The horses tore down the
grade that opened before them, stung by the
whip's bite, eyes rolling, mouths drooling
streams of stringing lather.

"Griswold, break out the express messenger's
goddamn Greener!" the gunfighter shouted
down. "Them riders are still gaining on us. Don't
give them no chance to come up alongside!"

Careful to keep to the inside, Tree urged his bor-
rowed horse to maintain its steady gallop. The
long upgrade had crested more than a mile
back, and he swung down into a vale between
ridge heights, stippled with white pine, spruce,
and alders — and away from slopes, great doug-
las firs. The trail then dipped through a foaming
creek. Emerging and climbing yet another slope,
rounding another curve, Tree could see the
quarry less than five hundred yards off, coach

swaying on its thoroughbraces, wheels spinning and boiling out the dust.

Tree spurred on, getting close enough to eat the coach's dust. Both stage and pursuer entered a high-walled gap. The rumble of the wheels echoed from the granite walls, and the rig rolled from the deep shade of the ravine into glaring sunshine.

Then a slamming blast of a ten-gauge scatter gun boomed out.

"Damn!" whooped the hangman. Griswold's blast had flown wild, and Tree was alive. He bent low across the saddle bows and spurred his mount into a last tremendous dash to within a few yards of the coach. Now Tree leaned and launched himself, grabbing onto the boot behind the racing wheel. Using every ounce of his strength, the hangman hauled up the vibrating cargo brace and locked a hand on the solid baggage bar. With another powerful pull, he rolled onto the roof, arms and legs splaying awkwardly.

Haldane glanced around and shouted down, "Griswold, the bastard's climbed aboard!"

On gut instinct, Zachariah Tree threw himself to the roof's side, and dug with fingers and boot toes the smooth oak wood.

With a bursting crash, the boards exploded upward, blowing the stage roof open in a hail of double-aught buck.

"I got the bastard!" roared Sam Griswold. "Blew him off'n the roof, and plumb to hell!"

"Showed that son of — " Haldane felt the hangman's hideout gun's .32-caliber slug. The tall gunfighter was thrown half around, and dropped the reins.

The four surging beasts got their bits between their teeth and headed off the road.

Haldane, clutching his drilled side, tried to scramble toward Tree, but slipped on the other side of the jehu box and fetched up with a grunt.

Out of control, the coach careened into a huge boulder and rebounded with a rending crash, and sprung sideways from a demolished off-front wheel. The door panel and sidewall both split lengthways, spilling seats, curtains, a shotgun — and one overstuffed, squealing man. Samuel Griswold bounced like a child's rubber ball on the flinty earth.

Seconds before the crash, Tree grabbed Haldane's arm and leaped off the roof with gun in hand, landing in a soft clump of gravel. But before he could turn, the gunman had jumped him from behind.

"I'll kill you, Tree," Haldane shouted, coming up with his good hand clenched in a powerful fist.

Tree rolled with that blow, blocked another, and swung at the gunfighter's jaw with his left. The punch powered Brace Haldane around like a kid's toy top. He went facedown in a mulch of rotting pine needles on his wounded side and groaned in pain, unable to move.

Seeing his man down, Griswold made a last desperate try for freedom. He plunged through brush, under tall firs, running and staggering. As he drove toward the forest's heart, his straining muscles failed him, and he fell in the mire of a creek's bank legs and arms flopping.

"I'm done!"

"Yeah, you're done, all right," Tree said standing over him. "On your feet, feller." Tree yanked him erect. "Get the stage horses. I'll bring Haldane."

"Brace ain't dead?"

Tree looked over at the downed gunman. "He'll live to hang."

For the first time Griswold's pink features lost their color.

"And you'll stand beside the gunsel on the gallows, Griswold."

"Name your price, Tree and I'll — "

Tree drove a fist to his mouth. There was the crunch of breaking teeth.

# Chapter Twenty

Tree stood among the clutch of lawmen, the preacher, culprits, and surveyed Deadwood from the high gallows' platform with steely eyes.

It's all about as familiar as can be, the hangman was thinking. A pair of murdering rascals on a scaffold. A street crowded with folks aiming to watch them swing. Circus day.

The man in the black coat, black trousers, and black hat tugged at his white shirt. He cast his eyes above the crowd's heads and the field of roofs off toward the towering, distant mountains. Today the sawtooth peaks looked blue. Blue peaks, blue sky.

Olive wore a red dress at her station down beside the hearse. She stared up at the gallows with an empty gaze.

# THE HANGMAN

Haldane and Griswold, the condemned men, stood stock-still, decked in dark cloth hoods.

Zachariah Tree stepped past the other observers on the scaffold floor, positioned himself near the culprits atop the traps, and waited.

Noise filled the air, the usual insults, the usual curses and jokes. No, they weren't going to be quieting down. They never did.

It was just some people's way. It had been a quick trial, but a fair one, with a new judge brought in all the way from Yankton, and a fresh jury. The verdict: guilty. The sentence: hang by the neck until dead.

The first two rounds had been stood by saloon owners to all after the case was over. Then celebrations raged all night.

Now, in the last few minutes before the execution, Zack Tree saw Rebecca Dunmore once more. She stood front row, center, as he looked from the gallows height at her.

The hour of high noon had come. Somebody, somewhere clanged a bell. Brace Haldane cursed beneath the hood. Sam Griswold whined like a cur.

Both culprits had foregone making their last-words speeches. It was a welcome relief for the audience. Good for the hangman, too.

A few Chinese men in conical black skullcaps lurked at the crowd's far edge. Blank faced and inscrutable this day, as always. And yet they were watching, not out working at their claims.

Tree's suggestion that the Chinese share in the bonanza strike had been hooted down. After the trial, it was discovered that Griswold's claim *wasn't* Griswold's claim. It belonged to a jasper named Hearst. Misplaced documents had surfaced. Claims-Recorder Donleavy returned suddenly back east, after inheriting a fortune from a lost uncle. Will Hearst would be moving over from the Comstock, where he'd made his first fortune. Deadwood was lucky to get him. He was a gent who understood the running of great mines. Now the crowd was out of patience, restless. Tree was out of patience, as well. He placed his hand on the planed-smooth trap lever. He glanced down — and met the Dunmore woman's firm gaze. She mouthed something, but the words were swallowed by the crowd.

Zachariah Tree looked toward the culprits and pulled the lever quickly. The heavy, well-lubricated traps dropped immediately, sending the two condemned men to a fast, painless death.

Finally, justice had been served in the town of Deadwood, Dakota Territory.

Tree teams up with a bounty hunter to clear four Blackfoot braves due to swing for gunrunning at Fort Sully, Montana in . . .


**AIR DANCE**